Other series by Perci

LUTHER (

This dangerously handsome, effortlessly stylish half-demon is Chicago's foremost paranormal investigator. With magical aptitude and specialized weapons, Luther Cross will handle your supernatural problems… for the right price.

THE MYTH HUNTER

All the legends of the world have some element of truth to them. And to track down those legends, there are the myth hunters. Some, like Elisa Hill, are explorers, trying to learn more about the world. And some are soldiers of fortune, whose only goal is profit and exploitation, no matter the risk.

INFERNUM

A shadowy, globe-spanning network of operatives run by the mysterious power broker known as Dante. They hold allegiance to no one, existing as rogues on the fringes of society. No matter the job, Infernum has an operative to execute it—provided you have the means to pay for it!

VANGUARD

The world has changed. A mysterious event altered the genetic structure of humanity, granting a small percentage of the population superhuman powers. A small team of these specials has been formed to deal with potential threats. Paragon—telekinetic powerhouse; Zenith—hyper-intelligent automaton; Shift—shape-changing teen-ager; Wraith—teleporting shadow warrior; Sharkskin—human/shark hybrid. Led by the armored Gunsmith, they are Vanguard!

Visit PercivalConstantine.com for an up-to-date list of titles!

Published by Pulp Corner Press

http://www.percivalconstantine.com

A MORNINGSTAR NOVEL

LUCIFER FOREVER

BY PERCIVAL CONSTANTINE

CHAPTER 1

A demon and an angel walked into a bar.

No, that's not the set-up for a joke. In this case, the demon and the angel were on the run from both the forces of Heaven and Hell, which left them few avenues to remain invisible.

The demon was none other than Lucifer himself. After centuries of living in isolation and ruminating over his failed rebellion, the Morningstar finally reached his limit and abdicated the throne. He attempted to retire to Earth, leaving behind the politics of Heaven and Hell.

It wasn't long before he got dragged back into those same politics, eventually ending in a trial in Hell where he was found guilty of betraying his revolutionary principles for his own self-interest.

His companion was Anael. Several lifetimes ago, they were lovers. But that was before the war and everything that followed. When Lucifer left Hell, it was Anael who was tasked to get him to return to the throne. It took some time, but soon, Anael learned it was just another attempt at gamesmanship on the part of Heaven.

Now they were both on the run. Anael had violated her orders by defending Lucifer in his trial and then refused to return to Heaven. Instead, she sacrificed any chance for forgiveness by aiding Lucifer in his escape.

Lucifer had conned Kushiel, Heaven's jailer, into helping them abscond. Then as soon as he brought them back to Earth, Lucifer killed him. It wasn't the proudest moment, but it was a necessary evil. They both knew it would only be a matter of time before the energy expelled by Kushiel's demise drew attention, and so they left Lucifer's home in Evanston's Lakeshore Historic District on the border of Chicago.

Their first stop was a dive bar in Englewood. Far from the most pleasant of neighborhoods in Chicago, but they needed the help of the man who ran his operations out of there.

Lucifer pushed the door open and the stench of smoke hit both him and Anael as soon as they entered. It seemed darker in here than the street. Conversations hushed when they saw the pair enter.

The bartender was tall and broad-shouldered. His eyes had a reddish tint to them and he gave a nod by way of welcome to the two.

"Mr. L., wasn't expecting to see you here tonight," he said.

"Erik, right?" asked Lucifer.

The man nodded. "That's right, sir." His glance turned to Anael and he focused on her unnatural blue eyes. Without breaking his gaze, he spoke again to Lucifer. "Though not sure why she's here with you. Boss hasn't had a good track record with *her* kind."

Anael tightened her lips, restraining her anger. Lucifer had informed her on the way here what sort of resistance they were likely to encounter, but she was on edge already and this wasn't helping.

"She's with me, that's all you need to know," said Lucifer to defuse the situation. "And speaking of your boss, we'd like a quick word with him. Just a few minutes of his time and then we'll be on our way."

Erik kept his eyes on Anael as he drew his phone from his pocket and sent a quick text. His phone beeped a few moments later with a response.

"Boss says you can go in," he said.

Lucifer smiled and slightly bowed his head. "Thank you, Erik. You're a gracious host."

"Sir, if you don't mind," said Erik just as Lucifer and Anael were about to head to the back room. "Belial hasn't been answering any messages. Was wondering if he was okay?"

Lucifer's face darkened, but he wouldn't give away the truth. "He's…wrapped up in something at the moment. I'm sure he'll contact you as soon as he's able."

They entered the door leading to Odysseus Black's office. A powerful sorcerer in his own right, he also had his hands in a lot of Chicago's supernatural underworld. Black sat behind a large desk and had a glass of rum in one hand and a cigar clutched between the fingers of the other.

"Well, well, the Morningstar himself gracing me with his presence yet again." Black glanced at Anael. "But I gotta tell you, Lucy, I'm not so fond of your company. Sure, she's easier on the eyes than Belial, but that's not enough to distract from the halo of self-righteousness."

"Okay, I've been playing nice, but I've just about had it," said Anael as she stepped forward.

Lucifer stepped in front of her before she could move any closer to Black. He stared into her eyes and whispered,

"I *know* you're on edge. But if we're going to get this done, we need his help, like it or not."

Anael stepped back and folded her arms over her chest. Her lips remained taut.

Lucifer turned to the sorcerer. "Odysseus, my friend. We're in a bit of an unusual situation."

"I figured somethin' must be up. Word on the street is that ol' silvertop is happier than a pig in shit up in that ivory tower."

"You're talking about Uriel," said Lucifer.

Black nodded. "He won't stop crowing about how this is the dawn of a new day and all that."

"Is he saying anything else?"

Black shook his head. "Nah, won't go into specifics, even when asked. Meanwhile, Mara has been holed up inside her office at Lust. Won't come out for nothin', it seems. Not even taking appointments. I know, I've tried."

"We're in something of a unique situation at the moment," said Lucifer.

"This something that Uncle Odysseus should be made aware of?"

Lucifer wasn't sure how much he should divulge. Black had provided him aid and comfort in the past, but he was also an unpredictable sort with no real allegiance to anyone other than himself.

"Anael and I are on a bit of a scavenger hunt, so to speak. We need quiet passage to some of the other realms."

"Which realms?"

"We have to go to three places. The first two are easy enough for us to access on our own. But the third is a little trickier, at least not without drawing attention."

Odysseus took a few puffs on his cigar as he studied

Lucifer's features. He exhaled the smoke into his glass, allowing it to linger on the surface of the rum before he took a sip.

"You gonna make me guess?" he asked.

"Alfheim."

Odysseus took another sip, then set the glass down on his desk. He picked up his cigar and leaned back in his chair.

"Pick a different place."

"This isn't a matter of choosing a vacation destination, Odysseus. We *have* to go to Alfheim."

"That's a very risky proposition," said Odysseus. "The fae aren't very kind to visitors. Especially not ones associated with Heaven or Hell. Don't think I gotta remind you of your history."

Lucifer shook his head. "No, you don't. But unfortunately, we don't have much of a choice in this."

"You gotta give me a little more to go on if I'm gonna help you out," said Odysseus.

"My house," said Lucifer. "It's a real nice piece of property and if you assist us, then once this is over, it's all yours."

Odysseus chuckled. "What would I want with a piece of real estate in some fancy-ass neighborhood like that? Cops'd be kicking in my door every day of the week and twice on Sundays."

"You don't have to live there, you can do whatever you want with it," said Lucifer.

"To get you passage into Alfheim, I'll need somethin' more than that."

"Belial, you've been satisfied with the work he's done for you?" asked Lucifer.

"Sure. Good worker, nice violent streak. Payments have

been a lot more regular when he's on the job."

"As you know, he's been splitting his time between the two of us, but once this is all over, I won't have need of his services anymore. He'd be completely available to pursue other avenues and I could convince him to become a permanent fixture among your entourage."

Odysseus nodded along while he puffed the cigar. "Okay, now we're gettin' somewhere. But it's still not worth the trouble of running afoul of the fae. Gonna need you to put a cherry on top."

"Fine, I have one more thing to offer," said Lucifer. "How much business does your product do in Lust?"

"A fair bit," said Odysseus.

"But you've got competition, don't you?"

"You know I do." Odysseus cocked an eyebrow. "What're you hintin' at, Nick Scratch?"

"I can't make any deals on behalf of Lust's management, but I do have a pretty good working relationship with Mara," said Lucifer. "You help us out, I can see to it that she grants your people exclusive distribution rights in Lust."

"You think she'd do that? Crack down on all dealers except mine?"

"If you give us what we want, I'm sure I can convince her," said Lucifer.

"She won't agree to a deal like that without a taste. What could you get her down to?"

"Fifteen percent of your take," said Lucifer.

Odysseus shook his head and held up two fingers. Lucifer scoffed.

"Two percent is pushing it, Black. What about ten?"

"With Belial on my crew, it'd be cheaper to muscle out

the competition."

"You only get Belial if you help me out, so I wouldn't bet on that."

Odysseus grumbled. "Five."

"Okay, I can get her down to five. But only if you do something else for us."

"Yeah, and what's that?"

"We're not very popular among either the halo or the pitchfork crowd at the moment. We need a way to stay off their radars while we go about our business," said Lucifer. "And nobody works a spell like Odysseus Black."

"You're really in it, ain'tcha?" he asked. "What sort of scavenger hunt are you two on?"

"That's not part of the deal. I just need to know that you can provide us with the protection we need."

"A concealment spell from both Heaven and Hell? I can work something like that, but you gotta be careful," said Odysseus. "Camouflage doesn't work so well if you run around screaming like a damn fool."

"Meaning?" asked Anael.

"Meaning that the more you flash those fancy powers of yours, the less effective the spell will be," said Odysseus. "You can manage some stuff—little bit of strength here, little bit of spellcraft there. But you gotta stay grounded and keep your powder dry. You start flashing your wings or whipping out soulfire weapons, the spell won't be much good to you."

Before coming to Englewood, Lucifer had already known that too much use of their powers would draw attention, so he'd arranged for a car. Anael kept quiet throughout most of the meeting, but once they got back into the car, she voiced her misgivings.

"Are you sure that was a good idea?" she asked.

"If you know someone else who can get us into Alfheim, I'm all ears," said Lucifer.

"You have to convince Mara to go along with this and then there's the matter of Belial," said Anael. "Or do I have to remind you that he's currently trapped in Hell?"

"It's *my* fault that he's there, so of course I haven't forgotten," said Lucifer.

"So to recap, we have to rescue Belial from Hell, convince Mara to go along with this deal, and then retrieve Khronus's pages from Purgatory, the Dreamscape, and Alfheim. And all of that has to be done before we have a hope of making the changes we need."

"You're forgetting something, Ana," said Lucifer. "We're going to change the timeline. So for the first time ever, we get to operate free from consequences."

Anael scrunched her brows together. "I'm not so sure that's how it works, Lucifer. This spell isn't a 'Get Out of Jail Free' card. Khronus said that it's not something to be trifled with. Everything has consequences."

"What consequences are there?" asked Lucifer as he started the car. "We go back in time, we change all of this from ever happening. Everything gets set right. And if by chance it doesn't work, then we can just do it again. We literally have all the time in the *world*."

CHAPTER 2

Belial hung naked, suspended by a crane over a large vat of boiling liquid. The sounds of the cracks and pops from the bubbling oil grew louder, almost anticipatory as the crane slowly lowered him towards the surface.

His body was already covered with burns and blisters from repeated attempts at this torture. But if anyone had expected a reaction from the demon, he gave none. His muscles remained relaxed as he hung loosely with his arms above his head, the restraints connected to the crane.

Belial's body lowered closer to the oil. He closed his eyes and took a deep breath. The heat from the oil already stung the sores on his legs. Slowly, the crane lowered him into the vat.

Legs first, the oil searing away what remained of his bruised flesh. The heat was the worst kind he could imagine. Belial's tormentor moved slow, giving his body plenty of time to adjust to the incremental insertion.

He was lowered further, now up to his sternum. The smell of cooking flesh filled Belial's nostrils. He kept his eyes closed, pushing the pain away from his mind, trying to shut down as much as possible.

Belial was lowered even further, this time up to his chin.

His tormentors didn't want him completely submerged—or at least, not yet. What they desired more than anything else was the savory sound of his pained screams.

He refused to give them that satisfaction. They'd tried numerous times with different methods since he'd been captured. The oil was just the latest method and they were on the third round with this.

Each time they rolled out some form of physical torture, Belial took it all in stride. He'd invented many of the methods they were using on him and knew better than anyone how to withstand torture for prolonged periods of time.

The crane moved again and now, Belial's head was completely submerged. He opened his eyes, allowing the oil to burn through the sensitive lenses. Show them how little he cared about the physical pain they tried to inflict on him.

Time wasn't exactly the same kind of concept as it was on Earth. Belial had no way of knowing exactly how long he'd been in that vat of boiling oil. Certainly longer than any mortal body could withstand.

When he was finally brought out, he was almost unrecognizable. His flesh was burned and hardened with a crisp shell. The crane turned, moving him from the oil and suspending him over another large vat. Cool waves emanated from the surface of this one, but he wasn't slowly dipped in. This time, the crane simply released him and his body plunged into the cold solution.

There was an immediate sense of relief as his burns instantly cooled. They allowed him to remain in that second vat for as long as it took for him to acclimate. They seemed to be able to sense when the pain had completely left his body, for at that very second, a compartment opened at the bottom of the vat.

Belial was sent down a chute, the liquid draining along the way. The chute ended on a soft mattress, which supported his body's weight and shape as if it were explicitly molded for him.

Soft hands gently turned him onto his chest. He couldn't see them, but he could feel their lithe digits and smooth skin as they slowly rubbed a cooling, soothing balm over his fried skin. They moved over every single part of his body, from the top of his bald head and all the way down to the balls of his feet.

When they finished, they turned him onto his back and he could see them for the first time. Two women were working on his body, with the most beautiful features he'd ever seen. They were naked as well, and they used their own bodies to rub the healing lotions onto his skin.

Belial closed his eyes, attempting to disconnect himself from their administrations. His body still responded physically to their touch, though. One of them took him into her mouth, sending even more physical sensations charging through him.

He knew this tactic. First, they try to inflict the worst physical pain imaginable. Then, they stimulate him with the most sensual of pleasures. With his senses ping-ponging between the two extremes, his rational mind would fade into the black and he'd be completely at their mercy.

The women knew their craft—if they actually *were* women. More than likely, they were simply magic constructs with no sentience or agency of their own. They tried to stimulate his erogenous zones in every possible manner, but Belial wouldn't respond to their touch. No amount of stroking, licking, or fucking could make him present in the moment. His conscious mind remained in a zen-like state of readiness, pushing aside all external stimuli.

When the women were done, they cleaned him up and dressed him in fine, silk clothes that felt soft and pleasurable against his healed flesh. For all intents and purposes, his body was put back together even better than when the torture had begun.

The women left through a door Belial hadn't seen before and disappeared after they walked through it. Belial stood from the bed and went to the spot from where they exited. Now it was just a white wall.

"I trust you had an…eventful morning?"

Belial turned to the new voice. Asmodeus sat on the bed with his legs crossed, his long, dark hair spilled over the crimson suit he wore. In his hand, the archdemon held a bright-red apple that he occasionally bit into.

"First the torture, then the pleasure," said Belial. "And now comes the pitch, correct?"

"Never let it be said that you're all brawn and no brain," said Asmodeus.

"This has all worked out great for you, hasn't it?" asked Belial. "You manipulate the Court and manage to prove your worth by prosecuting Lucifer's case, then once he's off the board, you eliminate Beelzebub so you can reclaim a seat on the Court."

"I really have no idea what you're talking about," said Asmodeus, even feigning a confused look on his face. "I'm simply a loyal servant of Hell, doing my duty to punish one guilty of regicide."

"Regicide." Belial scoffed. "That's rich."

"Beelzebub was a king of sorts. He had his own territory in Hell over which he held absolute control."

"Territory that you now control."

Asmodeus gave a sigh laced with theatricality. "Sadly, yes. The burden of rule has fallen to me. Beelzebub had no appointed successor, so the Court felt that with my experience as one of the first Hell Lords, I was best suited to take his seat. And one of my first acts as a newly appointed ruler is to seek justice for our dearly departed former master."

"I will hand it to you, Asmodeus." Belial leaned against the white wall and folded his arms over his chest. "You're so good at shoveling bullshit, I'm almost convinced you believe it yourself."

Asmodeus gave a chuckle. "Let's be real about this current predicament, shall we? Lucifer's day is done. Soon, he'll be nothing more than a footnote in the history of Hell. But you and I? We have the potential to grasp power for ourselves. And shouldn't we take that chance?"

"Eons ago, we both pledged ourselves to the Morningstar. And unlike you, I still maintain my honor."

"To what end?" asked Asmodeus. "Trust should be reciprocal. But with Lucifer, it's always been a one-way street."

"Lucifer has never betrayed us."

Asmodeus shook his head. "Still so convinced of his lies, aren't you? He never cared about us or about Hell. All he cared about was his own pursuits. The second I became inconvenient, he sided with the cambion against me."

"Have you forgotten that you were the one who took sides against Hell in the first place?" asked Belial.

"A means to an end, after I was abandoned to Purgatory by the cambion and my realm snatched from me by him and that whore, Lilith!"

Asmodeus's anger flared and the apple burned to ash as hellfire consumed his hand. He quickly calmed himself and shook his hand until the hellfire was extinguished.

"What would you do if you were in my position?" he asked. "Would you still honor your commitment to a savior who abandoned you, or would you take whatever opportunity for salvation that presented itself?"

"You already know the answer to that."

Asmodeus frowned and gave a knowing nod. "Yes, I do. Which is disappointing, to be frank." He stood from the bed and walked over to the same wall, leaning next to Belial. "By the way, did you know that Lucifer managed to escape?"

"Of course he did." Belial chuckled and pushed off the wall. He pivoted on his heel and faced Asmodeus. "Your plan's already falling apart."

"A setback, to be sure. Things would certainly be much easier if Lucifer were completely off the board, I'll grant you that. But wouldn't go so far as to say anything's fallen apart. Although, do you know what's curious?"

Asmodeus moved from the wall, closer to Belial. He leaned in and whispered into the demon's ear.

"Lucifer's running around free as can be, but his loyal aide is my prisoner."

Belial gave a scoff. "If that's the best you can do, then that's really pathetic."

Asmodeus pretended to be insulted. "You wound me, Belial. Whatever do you mean?"

"You think I don't see that you're trying to turn me against the Morningstar?"

"You're right, it was a foolish ploy. But I had to give it the old college try," said Asmodeus. "It is curious, though, don't you think? That every time you end up in a situation, Lucifer puts his own concerns ahead of you."

"I live to serve the Morningstar, not the other way around."

"A good king should address the concerns of his subjects, don't you think?" Asmodeus returned to the bed and sat on the edge of the mattress. "You left Hell behind to join Lucifer in his Earthbound adventures, even though you despise Earth. When Lucifer lost his powers, he put off trying to restore them, which forced you to take up a new job. And now, you've been imprisoned for the murder of Lucifer's rival, while he's off on adventures with his... companion."

"And which companion would that be?"

Asmodeus narrowed his eyes. "Oh...I think you can guess. Here's a hint." He held his hands together and flapped his fingers to mimic wings.

"Anael's with him?"

Asmodeus placed his hands on his thighs. "Seems she's finally taken the big F."

"She's fallen?"

"That's how Heaven is labeling her at least. Though of course she hasn't actually become a demon. No, that requires the so-called corrupting influence of Hell," said Asmodeus. "Although technically, Lucifer never truly became a demon himself, did he? So at least he finally has someone who can relate to him."

Asmodeus rose from the bed and patted Belial on the shoulder. "Ah well, I'm sure everything will work out in the end. No doubt Lucifer and his beloved are currently hatching a plot to spring you from Hell so the three of you can ride off into the sunset. What's that saying on Earth?

Ah yes, three's a crowd."

Asmodeus walked towards the wall and as he reached a hand forward, the door rematerialized. He opened it, but paused before walking through.

"Wait just a second…" He glanced over his shoulder at Belial. "Three's a crowd isn't considered positive, is it?" Asmodeus gave a chuckle. "Mortals and their silly little idioms. Enjoy your torture cycle, Belial."

The demon left Belial alone in the room. He knew this was all part of Asmodeus's plan to break him and he would maintain his resolve with that as his guiding principle.

But there was still an element of truth in the demon's words. Belial had spent his entire life serving Lucifer and in return, he'd been rewarded with a fall from Heaven, exile on Earth, and now imprisonment in Hell.

And what, exactly, had it cost Lucifer?

CHAPTER 3

The Dreamscape wasn't a normal dimension like Heaven, Hell, or the mortal plane. It only existed within the collective unconscious of humanity itself. Accessing it was easier than gaining entry to Purgatory or Alfheim, but because it wasn't a concrete dimension, that also made it more difficult to navigate.

Humans entered the Dreamscape whenever their conscious mind became dormant. But they only remained in their respective corner. Entering another person's Dreamscape typically required some sort of unique ability or spellcraft.

The catch for Lucifer and Anael was that there wasn't one person whose dreams they had to enter. They were about to enter the larger collective unconscious. Such a thing was rarely attempted because it was so unpredictable and risky.

"You're sure you want to start here?" asked Anael as she prepared the ingredients for the spell.

They were holed up in a vacant storefront just outside the city. The windows were boarded up and with a simple spell, the doors were open to them.

"Facing down whatever horrors lurk in humanity's unconscious mind is preferable to trying to deal with Thanatos or the fae, at least for the time being," said Lucifer.

"And what about Mara? You still need to tell her about the deal you've made with Black on her behalf."

Lucifer flinched at that mention. Mara may have been loyal to him in the past, but now that he was a pariah in Hell, there was no guarantee that loyalty would remain. He'd already seen firsthand with the likes of Beelzebub just how far a demon's loyalty could be stretched.

"I'm sure Mara will agree that this is for the best."

"If you say so…" said Anael, but her tone betrayed her lack of confidence in his assessment.

Lucifer ignored the tone and took a can of spray paint. He drew a sigil on the tiled floor, large enough for him to enter on his own. For this to work, he'd need Anael to act as his anchor in the physical world. Without her, he could easily become lost in the Dreamscape and have no way of escape.

The flip-side was that he'd be on his own with no back-up.

"Are you sure about this?" she asked.

Lucifer nodded, though he had his own doubts. He pushed those aside and stepped into the center of the circle. Lucifer got down on his knees and placed his hands on his thighs. He closed his eyes and took a deep breath. His wings emerged from his back as he began muttering the words for the spell in Enochian. It was a language he hadn't spoken since before The Fall. The words felt strange on his lips, but he was able to recall them in perfect clarity.

Anael chanted with him, her own wings emerging from her back. She raised her arms and a soft, azure aura of soul-fire materialized around her body. A line formed between her aura and the sigil, a visualization of the link that had been established.

Lucifer's words slowed and his wings slackened, falling limp at his sides. His eyelids slowly opened and he saw he was in the same storefront. But Anael was gone, and so was the sigil.

He stood and walked to the door. When he opened it, he was greeted not by the vacant parking lot or the darkened street. Instead, his eyes were flooded with bright sunlight as he stepped out into a wide, green field. Flowers of all kinds bloomed freely.

Lucifer moved through the natural landscape. He turned briefly to see where he'd come from, but the store was gone, no trace remaining. He moved through the field and held his hands out, his fingers caressed by the soft, tall grass.

It was peaceful and serene. Not another soul in sight. Strange, he expected the collective unconscious of humanity to be at least somewhat populated.

"And why would you think that, Star of the Morning?"

Lucifer realized he wasn't alone. He looked for the source of the voice, but it seemed to come from everywhere.

"Who's there?" he asked.

"Humans come to the Dreamscape in order to recharge themselves after long days of being among their kind. It's a place of solitude, not socialization. Maybe you'd understand just how significant that is had you not spent eons hiding in a tower."

"Whoever you are, I'm in no mood for games," said Lucifer. "If you have something to say to me, you can say it to my face."

"Testy, aren't we? Very well, if you insist."

There was a sudden rush of wind. Dust flew from the flowers and the ground, batting Lucifer in the face. But no, not dust. The particles were rougher and harder than that. They were more like sand. And Lucifer suddenly understood who he was dealing with, surprised that he hadn't realized it sooner.

The sand swirled, forming into a tall figure in front of him. It slowly took the shape of a tall figure with long, blond curls and dressed only in a robe. The figure was somewhat androgynous, with a body that appeared male but with soft, feminine facial features.

"So, the God of Dreams is indeed real," said Lucifer.

"'God' is a bit presumptuous. I'm more of a personification," they said. "You may call me Morpheus. And then you can tell me what you're doing in my realm."

"Something was hidden here long ago. I'm just interested in finding it and then I'll be on my way."

"Hidden *here*? Not in any specific dream?"

"That's right. Once I find what I'm looking for, I'll be on my way."

Lucifer started to walk past Morpheus, but they reached a hand and grabbed his shoulder.

"I'm afraid I can't allow you to do that."

"And why not?" asked Lucifer.

"Something hidden within the Dreamscape, but not any particular dream? There's only one fitting that description. You're after Khronus's pages, aren't you?"

"Not that it's any of your business, but yes."

"Those pages aren't for anyone's use. Certainly not a fallen angel."

"I don't think you understand what's at stake here," said

Lucifer. "There are forces within Heaven and Hell that are conspiring together."

"Even if that were true, an angelic slap-fight isn't cause for concern. This universe existed long before they arrived and it will continue long after they've destroyed each other."

"And what if they took it all with them? You said it yourself, you're the personification of the Dreamscape. That only exists if humanity lives. If all humans die out, then what happens to you?"

Morpheus scoffed. "You think I'm so petty as to put my own existence above the importance of something greater than myself? With those pages, you'd have the ability to mess with the very threads of creation. No being should have that power."

"Then why was it given to me?" asked Lucifer. "If no one should have this power, why did Khronus tell my friend where to find the pages?"

Morpheus cocked an eyebrow. "Khronus gave up the location of the pages? She did this willingly?"

Lucifer nodded. That seemed to disturb the personification of dreams. Their eyes fell as they contemplated the significance of this revelation.

"I'm sorry, but I don't believe you," they said. "This must be a trick of some sort."

"I didn't come for a fight. But if that's what needs to happen…" Lucifer's eyes burned like hot coals. Hellfire coalesced in the palms of his hands. He clasped them together and a flaming sword formed in his grip.

Morpheus just chuckled. "Oh, you arrogant little piece of celestial shit. If you think violence will solve your problems, then I'm happy to oblige."

Morpheus leaped into the air and swept their arms

forward. A wave pulsated forth. It flattened the grass and flowers before turning them to ash. That ash got swept up into the wave and buffeted Lucifer. The Morningstar instinctively wrapped his wings around his body for protection.

The bright sky blackened and where there was once life everywhere was now just a barren, desolate landscape. Lucifer's wings parted and he saw the personification of dreams hovering above him, their eyes glowing with dark power.

"You were given a chance to leave willingly, Morningstar. Just know that everything that comes from this point on is the result of your own actions. The Oneiroi aren't so forgiving."

Morpheus exploded into a flock of dark, winged creatures. Each was a kind of skeleton with obsidian skin stretched taught over the bones. Their wings were like tendrils of leather hanging off the frame. Within the hollow eye sockets were eerie, orange glows.

The Oneiroi dove straight for Lucifer. Their limbs were equipped with talons that were like razors matching the sharpness of their spear-like beaks. Lucifer readied his sword and swung it to meet the first ones that came at him,

Though he could fend some of them off, he didn't escape unscathed. The Oneiroi he'd dispatched managed to tear chunks of his flesh off as a consolation prize and there were many more, coming from seemingly endless directions.

Lucifer's wings launched him into the air. If he couldn't fight them, then at least he could try escaping them.

He flew with all the speed that his wings could muster, with the Oneiroi giving chase. The open sky made him too easy to follow. He had to find another way out.

If he escaped back to Anael now, he might lose the chance to find the page. Morpheus would be on guard if Lucifer tried to return at another time.

In the Dreamscape, walking through a door meant transitioning into another location. Though there were no doors here, Lucifer had another power available to him in the Dreamscape.

He dove towards the ground with the Oneiroi giving chase. Lucifer's wings wrapped around his body and he concentrated, his eyes pulsated. Hellfire lit along the edges of his feathers until he was the equivalent of a flaming meteor. Just before striking the ground, Lucifer vanished, leaving the Oneiroi alone in the desolation.

Lucifer rematerialized somewhere else. He'd taken a chance that teleporting in the Dreamscape would have the same effect as a regular door. And it seemed to work.

But now, he was in a different location. With crimson skies and twisted, misshapen architecture. A tall, smooth tower stood just ahead of him, almost defiant in how different it was from the rest of the landscape.

Lucifer would have been a fool not to recognize what was in front of him. It was his own tower in Hell, or at least his former tower. He assumed this must be Morpheus's idea of a joke. As if seeing what he'd built would have any effect on him.

He flew towards the tower, ready to face it head-on. Whatever games Morpheus had in store for him, Lucifer would gladly face them.

But as soon as he reached the tower, it suddenly vanished. A bright beam of light pierced the crimson skies, cooling the color. Lucifer looked up, surprised to see what the light brought with it.

Angels. An entire battalion of them, their soulfire blades burning with bright, azure light. They descended upon Hell, attacking it *en masse*.

"No..." Lucifer muttered, prepared to enter the fray himself. But then he heard the cries of the battalion's general, and the voice chilled him to the bone.

"Brothers and sisters, today we fight for the cause of Heaven! Today, we cleanse this blight upon the universe with the flames of purity unlike any the universe has ever seen! Today, we destroy Hell in the holy name of the Presence!"

The general of Heaven's divine army was none other than a beautiful man with dark hair and the symbol of the cross burned into his flawless chest. His eyes were the bluest that had ever been glimpsed and a grin of arrogant righteousness was plastered on his face.

The general was none other than Lucifer himself.

CHAPTER 4

Lucifer stood in shock as he watched some version of himself lead a battalion of angels in an all-out invasion of Hell. He hovered in the distance, away from the field of battle.

Morpheus is playing games, was the thought that came to Lucifer. The Dreamscape was their realm, and when not tied to any specific person's dream, that gave Morpheus all the more control over what was seen here.

Just like with every dream, what Lucifer needed to do was simply find a door of some sort. He could have tried teleporting again, but instead, he dove for the tower. Lucifer flew for the balcony near the summit. Once he landed, everything changed again in the blink of an eye.

Lucifer looked back from where he had come. What he saw was that he was standing on the veranda of a small beach house. He didn't recognize what beach it was, but this seemed to be the only house on the sandy banks.

A sound drew his attention inside. Lucifer opened the sliding glass doors and entered the home. It was a simple house, nothing extravagant. Modest decorations and furnishings.

The noise came from the second floor. Lucifer walked

up the stairs and now he could make it out. It was a sound that both disturbed and charmed him at the same time. He went to one of the closed doors and was surprised to see a bassinet swaying lightly. Lucifer approached it and looked inside.

A baby lay in the bassinet, its tiny hands held up, eyes scrunched together, and toothless mouth letting out a series of cries. Lucifer just stared at the child in wide-eyed amazement, unsure what to make of it.

"You know, she won't bite if you pick her up."

Lucifer spun at the sound of the new voice. It was Anael, leaning against the doorframe with a baby bottle in hand. She was dressed in casual clothes and her hair was simply tied behind her head. And yet, she'd never looked more beautiful in that moment.

He turned back to the baby. A girl, apparently. Lucifer reached his hands inside and lifted the child from the bed. He held her at arm's length, just staring in surprise. The baby continued crying in response. Lucifer looked to Anael for some help.

"What do I do now?"

"Try holding her like a baby and not some strange discovery."

Anael came over and showed Lucifer what she meant. She took the baby and positioned her head in the crook of Lucifer's left arm and then pulled his right arm down underneath to support the child.

"There, see?" Anael stepped back and smiled. "She's stopped crying."

Her eyes were wide open and she stared up at Lucifer. They had a kind of green glow to them.

"This…isn't possible," he said and looked back at Anael.

"Angels and demons can procreate with humans, but not with each other."

"Really?" Anael stepped beside Lucifer and rested her cheek against his shoulder while looking down at the baby's face. "Tell that to the creature that wakes us up every few hours in the middle of the night."

It of course made no sense. Lucifer handed the child over to Anael and then moved for the door.

"Lucifer, where are you going?" she asked.

"I'm sorry, but none of this is real," he said and stepped through the door.

Everything changed once he did. He was now in Lust, watching himself dressed in a suit speaking with a small group of young, beautiful women with him as the center of attention.

"What we're looking at are the different aspects of your personality, Morningstar."

Morpheus again, having suddenly appeared beside Lucifer. They passed him a glass of champagne.

"Your greatest fear, your greatest desire, and your greatest delusion."

"The greatest fear I understand," said Lucifer. "It's what my trial was all about, that I've become a pawn of Heaven despite myself. But the greatest desire and delusion are the ones that don't make any sense. You're saying I desire to have a kid with Anael?"

"I'm not saying anything. I don't create illusions, Lucifer. All I do is manifest what's in your subconscious."

"And my greatest delusion is this?"

"A kind of self-delusion, yes. The idea that all you want is to retire to a life of debauchery among the humans. Maybe that appealed to you once while you were looking at it in the abstract, but things didn't work out that way."

"I had responsibilities to attend to."

"Did you?" asked Morpheus. "Or did you simply want an excuse to do something with your existence? Perhaps you found the human world as boring and mundane as you did the role of king."

"You're a therapist now, are you?"

"Dreams are just a window to the subconscious. Understanding their meaning can tell you a lot about a person."

"I'm not interested in your games, Morpheus. I just want what I came here for."

"And as I told you, I can't give it to you," said Morpheus. "I'm not sure what you think is going to happen here, Morningstar."

The dream dissolved, like sand blowing in the wind. Now the pair stood in a desert that stretched as far as the eye could see, with the moon hovering above them and casting a soft light over the landscape.

"You can't fight me, you don't intimidate me, and your arguments mean nothing."

As Morpheus walked, a staircase rose out of the sand. With each step they ascended, another rose to meet their foot. Until finally, a platform rose from the sand, upon which a throne of sand was also created. Morpheus sat on the throne and looked down on the first of the fallen.

"You've lost this battle, Morningstar. You can either leave now or I can imprison you in your own nightmares. But I've long tired of your arrogance, thinking that the universe owes you anything."

Lucifer began to ascend the sand steps, but they dissolved. He fell face-first into the desert sand. Undeterred, Lucifer rose and shook the sand from his body. His wings emerged and raised him up to Morpheus's level.

"Very well, I'll leave," he said. "But I have a question before I go."

Morpheus nodded for Lucifer to continue.

"If I'm able to obtain the other pages, will you give me the one in your possession?"

Morpheus scratched their neck while they thought on the proposal. Finally, they said, "If you have the other pages, then that will buy you an audience to plead your case. But I wouldn't hold my breath if I were you, Lucifer. I still find it hard to believe that Khronus would trust you of all people with such destructive power."

"Then you'd be wrong."

"Khronus is older than any of us, perhaps even older than Death. And with her age has come greater wisdom than any of us possess."

"Hence why you should trust her judgment."

"I *do* trust her. It's *you* I don't trust," said Morpheus.

With a gesture, Morpheus commanded the sand. It formed into the three aspects of Lucifer they had seen—the warrior of Heaven, the simple father, and the aloof and irresponsible playboy.

"You don't even know who you are. Why do you think you'd be worthy of power over time itself?"

"I know exactly who I am and what I'm fighting for," said Lucifer. "I've made mistakes in my life and I'm trying to correct them."

"All creatures make mistakes. That doesn't give them the right to manipulate time." Morpheus waved their hand again and the aspects of Lucifer dissolved with a gust of wind. The sand they were composed of struck the

Morningstar directly in the chest and threw him from the platform.

But instead of throwing him down into the desert, the wind and sand pushed him up further. Lucifer was sent like a rocket into the sky until the darkness of the night enveloped him completely.

His eyes opened, and he was back in the vacant storefront, sitting in the middle of the sigil. Anael was with him and she looked at him with a start.

"That was fast," she said.

Lucifer stood and stepped out of the circle. "And a waste of time."

"What happened?"

"Had a little chat with Morpheus."

"Morpheus is real?"

Lucifer nodded. "And an asshole. They've got Khronus's page but won't hand it over."

"Why not?"

Lucifer thought about divulging the details of the three dreams Morpheus had shown him. But a voice inside advised him against it. Instead, he decided to summarize it as non-descriptively as he could.

"Basically, they said I'm not worthy of having power over time because I don't know who I am."

Anael's brow furrowed. "You sure that's all?"

"Everything else was just dream nonsense, no sense in dwelling on it," said Lucifer. "But they said that if we can get the other pages, then they'll give me another chance to convince them."

"Then we move forward. Purgatory will be a challenge, so Alfheim should probably be the next stop," said Anael.

"Which means we have to speak to Mara and get her to agree to Black's terms."

CHAPTER 5

L ucifer had lost count of the number of times he'd been to Lust, but this was the first time that he felt some apprehension when he walked through the doors. Convincing Mara to agree to Odysseus's demands was one thing, but he was a wanted man—by both Heaven *and* Hell.

As long as he and Anael kept their wings concealed and didn't use their powers, he was relatively confident the glamour spell he'd crafted to alter their appearances would suffice to keep them hidden.

So far, it seemed to be doing its job. The bouncer at the door didn't give them a second look as they walked through the main entrance. It was still relatively early, just after nine in the evening, and it was a weeknight, so the crowd was far smaller than usual. The dance floor had space to move around, there wasn't a line of people competing for the bartenders' attention, and getting from the entrance to the stairs was simpler than it had ever been.

Lucifer could sense the presence of demons and cambions mixed in among the humans. Some of the demons would cast furtive glances their way that went on a bit too long for his tastes. But none made a move against him.

"Maybe we should have just called instead of coming down here," said Anael.

"If I had her number, I would have," said Lucifer.

Anael was a little surprised by that. "You don't have her number? With all the times you've come by to ask for her help—"

"Exactly, I *came* by," said Lucifer. "I prefer face-to-face interactions and when you can teleport, who has the need for a phone?"

"What about when you were powerless?"

"Of course I relied on it then, but it was lost somewhere between the trial and being imprisoned in Gehenna. And who remembers anyone's phone number these days?"

They arrived on the uppermost floor and Mara's office. Anael sighed as she examined the two guards flanking the door.

"Demons, obviously. If you weren't Hell's most wanted, that wouldn't be a problem. So how are we going to get past them without drawing attention or using our powers?"

"There's one superpower that only works in this realm." Lucifer reached his hand into his jacket and took out his wallet.

"You *must* be joking," said Anael.

"Watch and learn."

Anael walked to the balcony railing and leaned against it, watching as Lucifer went to talk to the guards. She was skeptical as he chatted with them casually, neither of them knowing the man they were speaking to was the Morningstar. She watched as he shook each of their hands and noticed he passed some money to them while doing so. The guards were all smiles, laughing with him and after a few minutes, Lucifer waved her over.

She stepped away from the railing and approached, her head slightly cocked in curiosity. Once she came close enough, Lucifer linked his arm with hers and one of the guards opened the door for them.

"Unbelievable." She shook her head. "Amazing what people will do for a few slips of paper with no intrinsic value."

They were alone in the room and the door closed behind them. The glamour dissipated as soon as they were by themselves. Lucifer went to the bar while Anael walked over to the windows overlooking the club.

"They said she'll be here momentarily and we should make ourselves comfortable." After making himself a martini, Lucifer went to the couch and settled into the red, leather cushions.

Anael focused on the view of the club. She'd been here before, but she never took the time to just think about the environment. A place where sin ran free and people checked their morality at the door. It represented everything the Divine Choir had told her all her life was wrong. And now, she belonged here more than she did in Heaven.

"I hope we can make this quick."

The third voice was familiar to the both of them. Mara entered from another entrance, coming down from her adjoining apartment. But as soon as the spotted the pair, she stopped in her tracks.

"Holy shit…"

"Good to see you, too," said Lucifer.

"There were rumblings that you escaped. Anael's little scheme worked, huh? She was able to spring you from Limbo," said Mara.

"Funny story about that—she never got the chance.

35

Once I arrived in Limbo, Asmodeus quickly turned me over to Heaven."

"What?" Mara moved back a few steps, as if the words themselves had staggered her. "Asmodeus was working with Heaven?"

"With Uriel, to be specific," said Anael, turning away from the window.

"Guess you discovered that after I helped you," said Mara. "Thanks for the update, by the way."

"We had other things to worry about at the time, so I'm sorry we couldn't stop by," said Anael.

"Can you share now? The Court's been pretty quiet about this, which has led to a whole lot of speculation flying around."

"It's a long story, but first, we need some help," said Lucifer. "At least part of that help requires us to go to Alfheim, without alerting either Heaven or Hell of our travel. We've gone to Odysseus Black for help, but of course, he has a price."

"And that's why you've come to me." Mara sighed as she put the pieces together. "What does he want?"

"His concoctions are pretty popular among your clientele, but his dealers have competition," said Lucifer.

"Exclusive distribution, right?" asked Mara.

"And in return, you get a five per cent cut of his profits."

"You're forgetting about something else—what Black gets in return," said Mara.

"What does that mean?" asked Anael.

"If I were to give him exclusive distribution rights in Lust, that would also give him a very competitive edge in this town," said Mara. "Black has been trying to re-consolidate his power ever since that witch knocked him down a few pegs. A deal like this would be a big step in that direction. Do you really want someone like him having that much power?"

"The devil you know, Mara," said Lucifer.

"Cute," said Mara. "But also troubling. If Black starts acquiring territory like this, it's going to piss off some of the other gangs. I'm not saying it'll be a full-on war, but—"

"But that's something it could build to," said Lucifer.

Mara nodded. "Right. By making this deal, I'm effectively taking sides with Black against everyone else as opposed to remaining neutral. That's not really good for us. I doubt Lilith would agree to this deal and I'm just a proxy for her."

"One deal alone won't give Odysseus the control he desires. And this is just a temporary measure. You can find other ways to work around this, grant concessions to the others," said Lucifer.

"Say you're right. If it gets out that you had a hand in this, that could pose further problems for us," said Mara. "The politics of the Infernal Court are shifting. Asmodeus has a seat again and your conviction has made some of your former supporters there uncomfortable."

"Gotta love those fair-weather friends of mine."

"Criticize them all you want—Hell knows I have. But whether I like it or not, they're the demons calling the shots. Lilith's relationship with them was tense even before all this. She can't be implicated by associating with you—especially not with the company you're keeping."

Mara's eyes drifted in Anael's direction with that last sentence.

"You can hate me all you want, little demoness. But I'm the one who's actually helping the Morningstar."

"Oh, *now* you're helping him? Must be Tuesday."

Anael took a few steps towards Mara. "What does that mean?"

"Don't play the nobility card with me. We need a scorekeeper to track all the times you've gone from friend to betrayer."

"I thought we were past this. After all, it was *you* who helped me last time."

"I took a chance out of desperation, but I'm not so sure that was wise."

"Ladies, ladies, please," said Lucifer, standing from the couch and moving between them. "The room's already red enough as it is without the two of you spilling each other's blood."

He sipped his drink and set it on the table, then turned to address Mara.

"I understand your suspicions. But Anael has given me a gift that makes up for all our previous…disagreements."

"That's not why I did it," added Anael.

Lucifer took a breath. "Of course that's not why she did it, she was just sticking to her convictions. But she's helping me now."

"I'm sorry, my Lord, but that doesn't mean jack to me," said Mara. "I want to help you, believe me. But this isn't up to me. Lilith is my mistress and I have to do what's best for her interests."

"I understand that, I do," said Lucifer. "Think of it this way, though. What if any deals you made today would be gone by tomorrow?"

"Lucifer…" Anael began to voice her protest to him revealing too much, but Lucifer held up a hand. She restrained herself with a sigh.

"I don't understand," said Mara. "Breaking the deals would only make things worse."

"What if you didn't have to break them? What if they never happened?"

Mara stared at Anael. "Last time, you mentioned Khronus. Is that what he's talking about?"

"We can prevent a potential war between Heaven and Hell, fix the mistakes that were made in the past, and create a new world. One where there's not even a memory of all these problems."

Mara looked skeptical. "I'm not so sure that's how this all works…"

"Trust me, my dear. Any agreements you make now will be null and void by the time this is all over," said Lucifer.

"You really believe it's that simple?"

"You've trusted me this far. I'm just asking you to do it one more time. Just one, little deal and I'll be able to fix all of this so it never happened."

Mara glanced around the room, still silently contemplating his words. She was unsure of whether or not this was the right move, but she believed in the Morningstar, even if many of her kind had either lost or were in the process of losing that faith.

"Okay, you have my support," said Mara. "I'll reach out to Black personally and tell him that I've agreed to the deal."

"Thank you, Mara, I promise that you won't regret it," said Lucifer with a wide grin.

"But there's something I have to warn you about," said Mara. "If this doesn't work, then you may have torched whatever bridges you still have left in Hell."

Lucifer gave a nod. "Yes, I'm aware of the consequences."

Anael watched him as he spoke those words. They had the ring of truth, but she doubted if he even understood what he was promising. Was he truly aware of just how much he was risking? And Anael herself was beginning to doubt whether or not he understood the weight of this undertaking.

CHAPTER 6

I t had been some time since Asmodeus set foot inside Eden. Until recently, his presence here would have set off all kinds of alarms. But now that he once again held a seat on the Infernal Court, he was afforded privileges that were out of reach of the average demon.

But even with that privilege, his presence didn't go unnoticed. Asmodeus grinned at the sound of hushed voices and whispers the second he entered Heaven's pan-dimensional embassy.

The other patrons weren't the only ones who acknowledged his arrival, either. A red-haired angel in a white pantsuit approached him cautiously, clearly unprepared for one of his stature.

"Can…can I help you?" she asked hesitantly before adding, "Lord Asmodeus?"

"How kind of you to remember my title, my dear," he said with a warm smile. He reached a hand for her shoulder and she flinched at his touch. That fear…it had been so long since his very presence commanded such a reaction. "I'm here to speak to your proprietor."

"Yes, he's upstairs. He's been expecting you."

"Excellent. I know the way, so I'll take it from here."

Asmodeus gave a bow of his head to the angel and walked to the white steps leading up to a restricted level of the club. This was just a large, white room. Empty save for a bar and a balcony.

The current host wasn't the first, just the latest. Raziel was originally in charge, having kept the title for centuries. He'd since fallen. Then came Pyriel, who went insane and tried to transform the cold war between Heaven and Hell into a hot one.

Uriel had no intention of following in either of their footsteps. But recent events had made him nervous, hence the reason why he took a big risk by reaching out to the newly appointed Hell Lord.

"Uriel, my friend, my brother, my partner-in-crime," said Asmodeus with a bombastic flair as he came near the bar.

Uriel tossed back a glass of vodka, then refilled it. "You seem awfully chipper."

"And you seem intent on putting that angelic constitution to the test," Asmodeus noted. "How many of those have you had?"

Uriel downed his drink, then his shimmering blue eyes met the demon's. "You talking glasses or bottles?"

Asmodeus snatched the bottle before Uriel could pour again. Uriel's face contorted into anger, but Asmodeus calmed him by refilling the glass. Then the demon walked behind the bar and took a glass for himself, filling it up. He left the bottle for Uriel's continued abuse.

"You're in a mood," said Asmodeus. "Would have thought you'd be on cloud nine now that Lucifer is off the board."

Of course, Asmodeus had already heard the rumors of

Lucifer's escape. But there was no reason he had to let Uriel know just how informed he was.

"Aren't you wondering why I reached out to you?" asked Uriel.

"My understanding is that Heaven and Hell haven't had much in the way of diplomatic ties lately. I naturally assumed you were simply trying to re-establish those ties, as I used to parlay with Raziel on a regular basis."

Uriel chuckled and sipped his vodka. "Oh, Asmodeus. If I had my druthers, I'd drop a bomb composed of all the souls in Heaven right in the center of that pit of yours and then fill in the crater with something of more practical use to the universe, like an interdimensional parking lot. Or a Denny's."

"Harsh, but I respect your candor." Asmodeus leaned against the bar. "Then why did you call?"

"Lucifer. He's not off the board anymore. Quite the opposite."

Asmodeus was impressed. The angel was being far more frank than usual. He'd expected Uriel to try to keep this secret from him. But now he realized that what the angel really wanted was for Asmodeus to take care of his dirty work. He continued to play along.

"How's this even possible? Gehenna is supposed to be impenetrable."

"It is, which makes it all the more confusing."

"What did Kushiel have to say for himself?"

"Nothing."

"*Nothing?*" Asmodeus repeated the incredulous line. "He must have some sort of explanation for why he failed to watch over Gehenna's VIP."

"He has nothing to say because we have no idea where

he is," said Uriel. "He's not in Gehenna nor in any other realm. Heaven has lost all trace of him."

"That can only mean he's somewhere Heaven can't see or he's been destroyed. What about Anael?"

"Missing as well, so we can assume they're working together," said Uriel.

"And what do you plan to do about this?"

Uriel looked up from the bar and pointed at himself. "Me?"

"I went behind the Infernal Court's collective back to make this deal with you because you assured me you could keep Lucifer imprisoned. Seems you've failed in your end of the bargain."

Uriel reached out and grabbed Asmodeus by his jacket's lapel, then pulled him closer. "Are you threatening me, demon? Don't forget that you're only in your position because of me."

"Do you *mind?*" Asmodeus pried Uriel's hand off his jacket. "Cleaning out Heaven's stank is even harder than chocolate stains."

"Lucifer's not only a threat to me, but you as well," said Uriel. "If he's running free, how long will it take before the rest of the Court learns that your scapegoat isn't as guilty as you've convinced them?"

"The Court can be made to understand the concept of the ends justifying the means. But how interested would the Divine Choir be to learn that you've been cutting deals with demons?"

"Wouldn't be the first time it's happened."

"True, but doing so without their approval? That's a different story, isn't it?" Asmodeus took a sip of his drink. "For good or ill, the one thing the Choir values above all else is order and respect for the hierarchy. An angel acting without sanction is the highest transgression. So I think you'd have more difficulties than me should our little affair become public knowledge."

A guttural sound came from Uriel's throat. They both knew Asmodeus was right. Uriel was the one with the true disadvantage here. Even if the Court learned that Asmodeus killed Beelzebub, it wasn't as if he was a beloved figure among the Court.

But Uriel's actions had led to the possible murder of Heaven's jailer. One of the Choir's prized angels. They would certainly not be as forgiving.

"What do we do?" asked Uriel.

"If you'd simply kept that little bitch on a leash, we *could* have used her to get to Lucifer," said Asmodeus. "But *nooooo*, you just *had* to gloat and cut her loose. And with her gone, we've lost our greatest lead."

"What about Belial? You can break him, can't you?"

Asmodeus shook his head. "I've been trying, but he's one tough bastard. That combination of loyalty and willpower is rare, and really tough to crack."

"There has to be someone else. They can't keep running like this, sooner or later they'll have to reach out for help," said Uriel. "Who would they go to?"

"Anyone in Hell would be too big of a risk, so they won't reach out to Cross," said Asmodeus, contemplating. "Mara would be the next logical choice. Though what would their plan be, that's the question."

"I don't give a fuck about their plans, I just want them stopped!" Uriel slammed his fist on the bar.

Asmodeus finished his drink and set the glass on the

counter. He took the bottle and refilled it, then had another sip.

"You're pretty agitated. I take it the Choir already knows about this."

Uriel nodded. "They've tasked me with recapturing both of them and I have no clue how to go about it."

"We start by setting out feelers," said Asmodeus. "Heaven has agents on Earth. Start contacting them, have them be on the lookout for anything unusual. I'll send up some demons to possess a few humans and see if they can kick over any rocks Lucifer and Anael might be hiding under."

"And Mara?"

"She's under Lilith's protection." Asmodeus shuddered when he mentioned his former lover's name. "To avoid raising suspicions, I'll have to respect those boundaries and go through her. But I'm sure I can learn what we need to know."

Uriel's head slumped into his arms, resting on the bar. "I don't think I have to tell you what sort of punishment we're looking at if we don't see this through."

Asmodeus chuckled. "Uri, Uri, Uri. You really think we face the same level of consequence? I'm a Hell Lord. As long as I've got my silver tongue, I can keep enough of the Court divided to avoid any retribution from them. And Heaven wouldn't dare come after me—a direct attack on one of the Court would be viewed as an attack on all of Hell. But you?"

Asmodeus bent over and brought his head close to Uriel's. He whispered his next words.

"You're just a seat-filler. You have no real status in Heaven. The Choir has no qualms about punishing you."

Asmodeus finished the drink and started for the stairs.

"This is all on you, brother. So I suggest you remember which of us faces the higher stakes and act accordingly."

Uriel watched as Asmodeus began to descend. He squeezed the glass and it shattered, spilling what was left of the vodka all over his hand and dribbling onto the counter.

The angel wanted nothing more than to slice off the smug bastard's head and stick it on a pike as a warning to any others who might be tempted to cross him. And what angered Uriel the most about Asmodeus's arrogant words was their accuracy. Uriel was the one in the far more vulnerable position. He had to find a way to track down and end Lucifer and Anael once and for all.

But he couldn't do it alone.

"Wait," he called out.

Asmodeus paused on his step and turned back.

"I have a proposition," said Uriel. "If you're willing to listen, I think this could benefit the both of us."

CHAPTER 7

Mara made good on her word and spoke with Odysseus, striking an official deal with him for exclusive distribution in Lust. Odysseus followed up on his end of the bargain and used his own magicks to open a portal into the world of Alfheim.

The dimension that belonged to the fae had remained neutral for years. They'd departed from the Earthly plane a little over a century prior and had kept to themselves. The dimensional passageways between Alfheim and other worlds were more or less closed off to all but those who knew the proper spells. Fortunately for them, Odysseus did.

Lucifer and Anael passed through the portal and stepped into the middle of a vast forest. It was very different from the forests they'd grown accustomed to. The colors were far more vibrant and not simply limited to earthy tones like green and brown. The hues of the vegetation spanned the entire spectrum of available colors. And there was a kind of bioluminescence to the trees themselves that illuminated the forest so perfectly, Lucifer was surprised when he looked up at the sky and saw it was actually night.

He glanced over at Anael to see how she was reacting to

it. She'd never seemed particularly taken with any aspects of Earth. But in Alfheim, observing the beauty of this strange forest, her face displayed a look of wonder unlike any Lucifer had ever seen on her before.

"It's…" She hesitated to try to find the right words, then sighed when she realized she couldn't. "Incredible doesn't do it justice."

"It *is* quite beautiful, you're right."

Anael almost had to struggle to tear her gaze from the forest and look at the Morningstar. "You've been here before?"

He shook his head.

"How come you're not as impressed by it?"

Lucifer knelt down and put his fingers through a patch of grass, feeling the earth below. He glanced around at the bright colors and listened to the peaceful sounds of the forest.

"Maybe I'm becoming jaded in my old age. Or maybe I'm just too focused on the job." He looked back at her and smiled. "But it's nice to see you enjoying it so much."

"As beautiful as it is, we shouldn't waste too much time," said Anael.

"You know where to find the page?"

The angel closed her eyes and concentrated. Khronus had implanted the knowledge of the page locations in her mind. She knew the realms where they were located, but she didn't necessarily know precise coordinates. Now that they were in Alfheim, though, when Anael concentrated she could get a sense of where it was.

"I can feel it…" she said with her eyes still closed. "It's here, but…faint. Kind of distant."

"Do you know which way we have to go?"

Anael's wings emerged and she flew above the trees. Lucifer sprouted his own wings and followed her. There in the night sky, Anael slowly rotated in a hovering position, one arm held out with her fingers reaching. She finally came to a stop and all her fingers curled into a fist, save one which pointed off into the distance. Her eyes opened.

"There. That's where it's coming from."

"You lead, I'll follow," said Lucifer.

Anael's wings propelled her towards the source of the signal and Lucifer flew beside her, allowing her to stay slightly ahead.

The forest's reach was wide, ending only at the edge of a cliff that spilled over into waterfalls cascading into a roaring river below. Across the gap were large, mountain-like trees with massive growths that resembled mushrooms extending off the trunks.

They flew over the gap and it was then that trouble occurred. Lucifer was hit by something—what, he didn't know. But it came out of nowhere and caused his entire body to seize up.

His vision blurred and he felt himself falling. He tried to keep himself aloft, but his wings wouldn't respond to his commands. Anael called out to him, but her voice was muffled and far off.

Lucifer struck a hard and wet surface, then felt waves crashing over him. Took him a moment to realize he'd fallen into the river and the rapids now dragged him down the length of it.

He could feel his extremities again, but the current was too strong to allow his wings enough leverage to escape. Lucifer felt useless as he was taken by the river, the waves continually forcing him back under. He had to fight to break through the surface again.

The river rushed towards another waterfall just ahead, larger than all these smaller ones along the cliff edges. He tried to swim against the current, to free his wings somehow, but the water was stronger than him.

Just as he reached the tipping point, he was halted. Lucifer was suspended right over the drop, watching as the white rapids collapsed down into the body of water far below. He wasn't sure how far the drop was, but the distance wasn't insignificant.

Lucifer looked down at his torso and realized the thing that held him in place was a soulfire rope. He glanced behind and saw Anael hovering above, holding the other end of the rope.

He grabbed the rope and fought against gravity with his wings. And with Anael's help, they were able to pull him from the river's edge and up onto the cliff.

Anael's rope dissipated and she landed behind him on the side with the massive trees. Lucifer allowed himself a few moments to just let his muscles relax from the ordeal.

"What happened?" asked Anael.

He shook his head. "I have no idea. One minute, I'm flying with no problem, the next I'm falling. Something hit me, but I don't know what."

There was a sound in the distance. Lucifer and Anael reacted right away, their respective energies generating weapons for the pair. A flutter came from one direction, then another.

"We're not alone," said Lucifer.

"You think?" was Anael's sarcastic retort.

A blade flew from the cover of the grass. Lucifer spotted it before it came too close and struck it with his hellfire sword. Then an arrow came for Anael, which she deflected with her staff of soulfire.

"Whoever's there, you might as well show yourselves," said Lucifer.

A figure moved from the trees, like a rainbow streaking across the horizon. Lucifer could barely register its movement and certainly wasn't fast enough to stop it from delivering a blow. He staggered, a stinging pain in his chest. Lucifer looked down and saw his shirt had a tear across the front and a fresh cut on the flesh beneath.

The streak came at him again, and though he was slightly more prepared, still not fast enough to combat it. He was struck again, this time against the jaw and a bloody cut left on his cheek as a souvenir.

"We don't have time for these games." Anael plunged her staff into the ground and it exploded, sending out a soulfire wave in all directions. Everything caught in the radius slowed momentarily and that's when she saw their attackers.

They were moving slow enough now to be seen, at least three of them. Short of stature, no more than three or four feet tall, with pointed ears. They had gossamer wings and their skin was no single color, instead it was like a prism going between different shades.

Lucifer and Anael restrained the three attackers with ropes made from their respective energies, tying them down and leaving them restrained on the grass. The creatures struggled against their bonds to no avail.

Lucifer generated a hellfire sword and put it to the throat of one of the creatures. "I know there's more of you out there," he called. "Either you lay down your arms or I start stabbing."

Silence filled the air. Lucifer was growing impatient waiting and he pressed the tip of the blade against the captive's throat.

"You're about to find out just how serious I am," he warned.

"Hold!" came a voice from the trees. Lucifer pulled the tip away from the captive's throat, but still kept the sword pointed at him.

More of the creatures flitted out from the trees, moving into the light where they could be seen. All of them had the same gossamer wings and prism-like skin as the three captives. Their armor, if it could be called that, was composed of leaves and tree bark. Their weapons seemed carved from wood and stone.

One of them moved forward. He was the largest of them, but still only about four feet tall. He had broad shoulders and his face was adorned with a bushy, orange beard.

"Who are you?" asked Lucifer.

The leader remained silent. Lucifer pressed the tip of the blade against his captive once again and this stirred the leader to action.

"I am Kelan of the Royal Guard," he said.

"Okay Kelan of the Royal Guard, just why did you attack us?" asked Lucifer.

"You're outworlders. Alfheim is for fae only," said Kelan. "Do you allow intruders to just waltz into your domain without repercussions?"

"We weren't aware that we were trespassing," said Anael. "You could have simply talked to us before attacking."

"Our experiences with outworlders haven't been what

you'd call positive," said Kelan. "Who are you and what's your purpose?"

"Someone we know left something here, we've been asked to find it, that's all. She's Anael and I'm Lucifer."

Kelan's eyes widened and then one squinted at the mention of Lucifer's name. He stared at Lucifer, his eyes passing over his body from head to toe.

"The Morningstar?" Kelan then scoffed. "I thought you'd be taller."

The irony of someone of Kelan's stature commenting on Lucifer's height wasn't lost on the fallen angel, but he held his tongue nonetheless.

"Kelan, we're not interested in any trouble. If you let us go, we'll get what we came here for and then we'll return to our world," said Anael.

"I can't allow that," he said.

"And why not?" asked Lucifer.

"Anything already in Alfheim's borders should remain within Alfheim's borders. If you wish to remove something, you need royal permission," said Kelan.

"That's fine, we can talk to the king," said Lucifer. "Oberon, right? I've never met him, but I know him by reputation. And I assume he knows me."

"Oberon is no longer king," said Kelan. "You must speak with Queen Titania."

"The queen is fine, we'd be happy to have some words with her," said Lucifer.

Kelan studied the pair, clearly untrusting of their true motives. "Tell me why I shouldn't simply kill you both where you stand."

Lucifer glanced back at Anael. He had one potential avenue, but he'd been loathe to try it. Alfheim was cut off from other dimensions, so it was very possible he could get away with it.

"You know my name, Kelan. So I assume you also know my title—I'm a king myself, or have you forgotten?"

Kelan narrowed his eyes. Lucifer steeled himself for the possibility that the fae would reveal he knew the Morningstar was a fugitive with nothing left to his name. If that happened, Lucifer started calculating how and if he and Anael could kill all these fae warriors and escape.

"I forget nothing, King of Hell," said Kelan.

"Good, then you know just what sort of a crisis Titania would have on her hands if you killed me. I doubt she's interested in an interdimensional war. Say that happens, just what do you suppose she'd do with the fae responsible?"

Kelan seemed to grasp the implications without problem. "Very well, Morningstar, you have your audience. I'll take you to the Queen and allow her to decide your fate."

Lucifer nodded, maintaining a steely resolve. Behind that mask, relief washed over him. He was taking a chance and judging by Anael's cautious and concerned expressions, he wasn't the only one who thought so. How long he could keep this charade going was another question. Though Kelan clearly wasn't up on current events, that was no guarantee Titania was the same.

CHAPTER 8

The Royal Guard took Lucifer and Anael prisoner temporarily until the queen was ready to meet with them. The pair decided to acquiesce to the demands of Kelan, albeit temporarily, and were escorted to the large trees they had seen earlier.

A gap between the roots at the tree's foot fed into a cavern. It was here that Lucifer and Anael were told to wait with several fae warriors left to stand guard. Their cell was made of stone with a boulder serving as their door. The ceiling was just under seven feet in height, leaving very little clearance for them. No torch was provided, but Lucifer was able to create a simple orb that gave them a light source in the pitch-black of the cave.

"Are we any closer to the page?" asked Lucifer once they were alone.

"It's nearby, I know that," said Anael. "My question is what will Titania want in return for it."

"Or if she'll want anything at all," said Lucifer. "If she's anything like Morpheus, she may not be willing to part with it."

"Maybe we're going about this all wrong, trying to ask for permission," said Anael. "We're far from Heaven's gaze, we shouldn't have any problems using the full extent of our powers now."

"Teleporting without a clear sense of where you're going, especially in an unknown realm, is a risky proposition," said Lucifer. "You might end up inside a mountain or a tree or even one of the fae."

"Point taken. And here I thought this would be the easy part of this mission."

"Just be patient. Everyone has a price and once I learn what Titania's is, it's just a matter of finding a way to pay it."

"More promises you don't intend to keep?"

Lucifer's head jerked to attention. "That sounds like a not-so-subtle accusation."

"How often have you made promises without considering the follow-through?" she asked. "You consider yourself a man of your word, but is that really true?"

"I've always strived to keep my promises to the best of my ability. Circumstances aren't often considerate of intent."

"I seem to recall a saying about roads paved with good intentions."

Lucifer sat against the far wall and rested his head against the stone. "What would you do in my position, Ana? We needed some way to get our hands on those pages."

"I'm not criticizing you."

"Could've fooled me."

"These are things you should consider. If you're always promising the moon and then failing to deliver, you'll eventually have to deal with consequences of those actions."

"If you've got a better idea, then I'm open to hearing it."

Anael sighed. She didn't have one, but that wouldn't do much to quiet her own reservations. "I'm just concerned, that's all. You've always seemed to consider that there's some magic bullet to solve your problems. It's been your guiding star even before The Fall. You're still chasing that impossible dream, even now."

There was a low grinding noise and a rumble, and then light came from a new source. Their cell was open and Kelan stood where the boulder once was.

"Queen Titania has agreed to grant you an audience," he said. "She's quite keen to meet the Morningstar in the flesh."

"And I'm keen to speak with the Queen of the fae." Lucifer stood and approached the exit, but Kelan wouldn't move.

"A word of caution," he said. "If I get the slightest sense that you pose a threat to the queen in any way, shape, or form, I will not hesitate to relieve your body of that meddlesome head."

"I'd expect nothing less of a Royal Guardsman," said Lucifer.

Kelan regarded Lucifer carefully, then stepped away from the entrance. Lucifer and Anael stepped out of the cell to find several other guardsman waiting with spears and swords already drawn.

"Follow me. And watch yourselves. Once again, the slightest misstep is all that it will take," warned Kelan.

"We understand," said Anael.

Kelan grunted and turned without another word to lead them forward. They left the cavern through the same tree roots and unsheathed their wings to lift them up. Lucifer and Anael did the same, flying after them, rising up the length of the massive tree.

It was easily the size of a mountain on its own, certainly as tall. They could now see that the mushroom-capped growths that came off the branches were actually homes and buildings. The fae civilization seemed completely integrated with the environment, nothing standing out as unnatural.

They rose up past the branches and found more homes. Lucifer guessed there were at least a few hundred who lived just in this one tree. And once they reached the summit, there was a larger cap here, in the midst of the multicolored leaves.

Kelan landed first and Lucifer and Anael next with the guardsmen remaining behind. Other guards waited for them and took over from the ones that stayed back.

Mossy ground rested beneath their feet and willows hung before the entrance. They parted as if by magic, giving way to a large, open courtyard. Lucifer marveled at the size of the place. Seemed far larger than the outside would suggest.

Fae were gathered in a large semi-circle, providing a clearing that Kelan led them into. He stopped right in the center of this circle and Lucifer looked at the prism-like eyes of the fae that surrounded them. All of them regarded the pair with suspicion.

Branches and vines lowered from the ceiling, seeming to grow out from their housings. A flower was here and the petals parted to reveal a woman with her multicolored hair done up in a beehive-like fashion, and wearing a dress of leaves. Her wings fluttered behind her, and her eyes shimmered with a spectrum of colors as she took in the two.

"Welcome to my home. It's been some time since we

had guests from another realm. I am Titania, Queen of the fae."

"Your Majesty, it's an honor." Anael crouched down on one knee.

"Yes, we're grateful you've granted us an audience." Lucifer's tone was submissive, but he remained standing tall.

"You don't kneel before a queen?" asked Titania with a cocked brow.

Anael shot him a look and Kelan stepped towards him, the fae's hand resting on the hilt of his sheathed sword.

"You know of me, I assume," said Lucifer. "Then I also believe you know that I swore to never bow before anyone again."

Titania raised a hand to her face, her long fingers dancing on the edge of her chin in thought. After a moment, that hand made a gesture to Kelan. The guardsman's hand fell from his sword and he bowed his head as he stepped away from Lucifer's side.

"I respect your conviction and will not take it as a sign of disrespect," said Titania. "Now, what brings you to Alfheim?"

Anael rose to her feet. "We're seeking something. A page of a spell."

"And what makes you believe it's here?" asked Titania.

"The location was provided to me. Even now, I can sense its presence."

Titania stared at the angel and then she cast a look in Kelan's direction. She gave a nod. At that silent command, Kelan flew above and drew all eyes in the court up to him.

"The Queen has demanded a private audience. All gathered must immediately depart!"

The gathered fae did as they were ordered and one by

one, filed out of the courtyard. When all had left, it was just Titania, Lucifer, Anael, and Kelan who remained.

"You as well, Kelan," she said.

"Your Majesty?"

"Do not make me repeat myself."

Kelan hung his head in shame and then knelt. "By your leave."

Once the guardsman left, it was just the three of them. Lucifer looked around the empty courtyard for sign if there were any stragglers.

"Don't want anyone else to hear what you have to say, huh?"

Titania stepped off her flowery throne. She stood at just over four feet, perhaps the tallest of the fae they'd seen so far. Her wings raised her up to Lucifer and Anael's eye level.

"Khronus sent you, didn't she?"

"Then you know what we're talking about," said Lucifer.

"That spell is quite dangerous. When Khronus entrusted it into the care of my late husband, she was quite specific about its importance," said Titania. "I'm the only soul in Alfheim that even knows it exists."

"As you said, Khronus sent us. It's how we knew to come here and how I can sense the spell is close," said Anael.

"Khronus also said that it would ultimately be up to the discretion of the guardian of the page whether or not to hand it over," said Titania.

"And you're not going to hand it over without getting something in return, are you?" asked Lucifer.

Titania smiled at the Morningstar. "You're very perceptive. I'd be a fool to simply give it to you without getting something for my troubles, wouldn't I?"

"What do you want?" asked Lucifer.

Titania held up her hand and blew into the palm. Dust particles flew into the air, forming into the image of a fae man. He sported a mohawk and had a mischievous grin on his face.

"This is Puck. Once a loyal servant of the court until he betrayed Oberon and killed him. Now he leads a rebellion from the far lands of Alfheim," said Titania. "Bring me his head and I'll give you what you seek."

Lucifer studied the features of the fae rebel. He noted a concerned expression on Anael's face, which he'd consult her about later.

"Consider it done," he said.

CHAPTER 9

I t was rare for Odysseus Black to find himself the subject of a summons. Usually, people came to him asking for an audience. Almost no one told him to appear somewhere on his own. But some still had that ability, which was why his limousine was currently rolling to a curbside stop in front of the Willis Tower.

Odysseus climbed out of the back seat and ordered his men to stay nearby. He didn't want to draw too much attention to himself in this instance. As one of the biggest players in the supernatural underworld, he had an image to maintain. Obeying a summons would tarnish it.

There weren't many reasons he found for coming to Eden. Heaven usually left him to his own devices and most of his business was conducted in the realm of sin anyway. Though he was neutral in their little tiff, he certainly had more in common with the denizens of Hell.

On the few occasions he did have to come to Eden, it was usually more lively than it was when he stepped off the elevator. Just a few scattered people were in the place, no one really of note. Odysseus thought he might have arrived too early, but then he remembered that time wasn't really much of a factor in this interdimensional post.

Uriel stood out on the balcony in a white suit, sipping a glass of champagne. Odysseus gave a quick look around and then strutted out to the balcony to meet the proprietor. He didn't give a friendly greeting of any kind, just walked to the railing and looked out over the swirling dimensional energy below. Odysseus took a cigar from his coat pocket, removed it from its case, and snapped to generate a small flame on the tip of his thumb. He puffed on the cigar as it lit, then shook his hand to extinguish the fire.

"I don't like being summoned, halo," he said.

"Fair enough. I don't like dealing with your kind," said Uriel. "But I need information and I understand you're a man who traffics in exactly that."

"An' just why would a halo need to sully himself by asking the likes of me for information? You boys seem pretty tuned into what happens in the world."

"My sources have informed me that Lucifer was seen in your neck of the woods," said Uriel. "I find that interesting when he was supposed to be imprisoned."

Odysseus gave a chuckle. "Guess this should be a lesson to you about arrogance. You were all exuberant about how wonderful things were now that the Morningstar was gone. Didn't seem to take, did it?"

"There's only one reason Lucifer would be in Englewood and that's to meet with you. No use denying it, Black, so just tell me what he wanted."

"Let me tell you a story." Odysseus took a few puffs of his cigar before he began. "Not too long ago, a certain captain of industry came to me, wanted me to help him get rid of a problem. See, he had this habit of…how do I put this delicately…imbibing in certain substances off the bodies of women of questionable moral character. And he learned that some tabloid reporter had gotten wind of this. He came to me to solve his problem, and it wasn't just because I could create a spell that made the reporter decide he'd be much happier as a conflict journalist in Syria. But it was because my client knew I understood the value of discretion."

"I assume there's a point to this story?"

"The point is that if I can't offer my clients discretion, then I'm not much good to them. So even if Satan came by my place, I wouldn't be able to tell you if he did and I certainly wouldn't be able to tell you what he wanted of me."

"So I see." Uriel finished the champagne and set it on the railing. A moment later, it magically refilled and he picked it up again for another sip. "Since I allowed you to tell your story, perhaps you'd indulge me for one of my own?"

Odysseus shrugged. "Knock yourself out, flyboy."

"This story is about a certain centuries-old sorcerer. Someone who fashioned himself a nice little business in modern-day Chicago. His clientele included not only the rich and the powerful, but also people out for the high that only his potions could provide."

"Sounds like my kinda guy." Odysseus gave a big laugh.

Uriel smirked and then continued the story. "Yes, this sorcerer believed there were few heights he couldn't reach. But he seemed to forget the one lesson that Lucifer's story should have taught him—that pride comes before the fall. And oh, this sorcerer was *quite* prideful.

"And then one day, a renegade angel came to him and offered him even greater power if he'd provide help. The sorcerer—who again was so certain of his invincibility—

thought this would be a simple matter. And so he agreed to help the renegade."

Odysseus frowned as he listened. He had a pretty good idea of where this story was going, and it wasn't a direction he favored.

"But, as is always the case in these situations, the sorcerer ended up being humbled. By some upstart young witch, nonetheless. She humiliated him in his own city, made a mockery of him.

"Since then, the sorcerer has limped on, trying to regain some measure of his former status. And though he's managed to make some headway in that department, he's nowhere near what he once was."

"I see what's happening here." Odysseus punctuated his words by waving his cigar. "You think you can get me to sing in exchange for Heaven's help in getting back what I lost, maybe even taking out some revenge on that witch?"

This time, Uriel laughed. "Oh no, no, you misunderstand me. Heaven *must* remain very hands-off in that department. If our divine hand were felt too strongly on Earth, it could endanger the armistice with Hell." Uriel sipped his champagne again. "No, the problem, Mr. Black, is you sided with a renegade angel. And instead of punishing you, we allowed you to get off without facing any consequences."

"Now hold up just a minute. I had no way of knowing that Pyriel wasn't on the level. Far as I knew, he was just doin' what your bosses told him to do."

Uriel held up a hand defensively. "Oh, I know. No one believes otherwise, Mr. Black. As you so accurately stated, you had no way of knowing…"

68

Odysseus now started to feel a sinking pit in his stomach.

"However," Uriel continued, "you still did it. And that caused quite a lot of problems for us. In fact, one might say that Lucifer never would have abdicated the throne and caused all this trouble in the first place if not for those events that transpired."

"You can't blame me for Lucifer."

"Blame *you*? Of course not, that's a ridiculous notion," said Uriel. "In fact, it speaks to the gregarious nature of Heaven that we allowed you to escape without punishment.

"And that also brings us to another problem. If we allowed everyone who spat in the eye of Heaven to just walk away without consequence, well, that would set a pretty poor precedent, wouldn't it? After all, how could we be taken seriously?"

Uriel narrowed his eyes and they hummed with soulfire. "You're crossing us again, Mr. Black. And we simply can't allow that to continue. So the way I see it, we have a few things we can do here. The first option is that you remain defiant and certain accidents start to befall you. As an example, the fundamentalist crowd has recently gotten into one of their periodic satanic panic modes. It wouldn't take much to direct them to someone like you."

"You think Bible-thumpers scare me?"

"No, not at all. But I believe their allies in the halls of power *do*. Just how useful would your discretion be when you have a target painted on your back and are the subject of a witch hunt?

"But that's just one option. Another is that you could lose your much-vaunted powers. It's one thing to be a sorcerer with no clients, it's another to be a sorcerer that can't deliver."

"You can't do that," said Odysseus. "You don't have that kind of power."

Uriel grinned. "We're *Heaven*, Mr. Black. We can do whatever we damn-well please. If I felt so inclined, I could make it so you believed you were a prepubescent little girl in Victorian England."

"And I'm going to assume that option three is the one where I tell you what I know about Lucifer," said Odysseus.

"If it makes you feel any better, you don't have to think of it as betraying a client's trust. Instead, consider it an insurance policy on your own business," said Uriel. "Every business needs an insurance policy in case something… unpleasant transpires."

Odysseus sighed and leaned against the railing. He puffed the cigar as he stared out into the void of this pocket dimension. "I don't know much."

"I'll be the judge of that," said Uriel. "Just tell me what you *do* know and then figuring out my next step will be my responsibility."

"He was with Anael and they wanted secret passage into Alfheim."

"The fae dimension? To what end?"

Odysseus shrugged. "All I know is they were lookin' for something in there. What it is, I got no clue. And he also asked for a protection spell so they could stay off both Heaven and Hell's respective radars."

"Tell me more about this spell. What it is and more importantly, how to counter it."

CHAPTER 10

Titania had provided a general idea of the vicinity in which the rebels were known to occupy. It was far from the capital in what she called the Dark Forest. Even with the aid of flight, it would still take at least two days to reach the area and begin their search.

Few words passed between the two on that first day of flying. It wasn't until they landed and made camp for the night that they finally had an opportunity to speak. Lucifer had been focused on the task, trying to work out just how he'd complete this mission. But Anael? Her concerns were different.

"Are you ready to tell me your real plan?" she asked as they finished gathering wood for a small fire. Anael used her soulfire to conjure the campfire and then sat near it.

"I won't be sure of the specifics until we actually get there and see what sort of force we're dealing with," said Lucifer. "Though judging by what Titania and Kelan have told us, they're guerrilla fighters."

Anael shook her head. "I don't think any of Titania's people are around. You can tell me your *real* plan now."

Lucifer's brows scrunched together as he tried to decipher her meaning. "I just told you. If you want something

71

more detailed, I honestly haven't thought that far ahead."

Anael hunched forward. "So you're seriously going to go through with this?"

"Why wouldn't I?"

Her jaw slackened as she studied the face of the man she thought she knew. "You're unbelievable."

Lucifer blinked several times in rapid succession. "I'm sorry, are we resuming a fight that I didn't know we were having?"

"You were once in Puck's shoes, or did you forget when you staged a rebellion of your own? And now you're going to condemn him for the same action?"

"Now hold on a minute. First, I seem to recall you being very much opposed to that rebellion. Second, the rebellion was never my idea. My hand was forced," said Lucifer. "Third—and arguably most important—just because there's a rebellion doesn't mean they automatically have the moral high ground. There have been numerous revolts in human history led by absolute evil bastards."

"And how do you know Puck is another example of that?"

Lucifer was at a loss for a response.

"You see? You don't even know the full story, and yet you're ready to assassinate him just on Titania's word."

Lucifer grimaced. "I'm not saying you're wrong…"

"I sense a 'but' coming."

"…but what other course of action do we have?" he asked. "We need that page, Anael. Without it, we can't go through with this.

"I understand that."

"If you have a better plan, then I'm willing to entertain it. This is all we have, and I should remind you that this was your idea," said Lucifer. "So if you know some other way to get our hands on what we need, then don't hold back."

"I just want you to consider the consequences of the actions we're taking," said Anael. "You're charging head-first into these situations, making moves without any concern for the results."

"It doesn't matter. We're going to go back in time and undo everything that happens here."

"You keep saying that, but it doesn't make it true," said Anael. "There's so much we don't know about time. As far as we know, no one has ever attempted something like this before, and Khronus didn't exactly provide a rulebook."

"Exactly my point," said Lucifer. "You'd think that the master of time would be more concerned about these potential consequences if they existed. The fact that she *didn't* give you a list of dos and don'ts tells me you're getting worked up over nothing."

"She warned me that if we're not careful, we could end up doing greater damage."

"I really doubt killing a revolutionary and cutting a deal with a petty sorcerer will unravel the fabric of the universe," said Lucifer.

"I'm not sure that's a chance we should take," said Anael. "At the very least, let's learn more about this rebellion and just what it means.

Lucifer nodded. "Okay, we'll do it your way. But I think you'll find in the end that we don't have a whole lot of options."

LUCIFER FOREVER

After getting some rest, Lucifer and Anael returned to their flight early the next morning, just before daybreak. Just a few short hours after they resumed their flight, the skies darkened very quickly.

"This must be why it's called the Dark Forest," Lucifer noted. "Seems we're in the right place."

They descended to the trees below, passing through the foliage and hovering just above the ground. Lucifer closed his eyes and concentrated, reaching out with his senses to get a feel for where they should go from here. His power reached out, stretching through the forest. There were several signatures in the vicinity, but none in particular stood out.

"Looks like we found them," he said to Anael in a hushed tone. "Or rather, they found us."

Before he could say another word, something sprung from the bushes and struck him from behind. It moved like a green blur, flipping in the air and then disappearing into a shrub.

"We're not interested in a fight," said Anael. "Can we talk?"

"So you think the Puck's a fool?"

The voice echoed in the forest, making it impossible to determine its origin.

"Puck knows you met with the false queen."

"No lies, no tricks," said Lucifer. "Yes, we met with Titania. But now, we'd like to meet with you."

"Angels aren't known as friends of revolution."

"No, they're not—but I am," said Lucifer. "Surely the Puck has heard of the Morningstar?"

No echoing voice replied. The forest grew still for a pregnant moment. And then, rustling came in the leaves above.

That green blur moved again in the trees, ping-ponging between them before finally landing in front of the couple in a crouched position.

Unlike the other fae, this one didn't have any wings to speak of. He was just as short, but his limbs looked to be longer than the other fae they'd met so far. His face had sharp angles and there was a spark of mischief in his eyes, with the tip of his dark mowhawk threatening to obscure his vision.

"Of course Puck knows Lucifer," he said. "And he's pleased to make your acquaintance."

"You're Puck?" asked Lucifer.

The elfish man nodded and stood upright, then bowed theatrically. "At your service."

"We'd like to have a discussion with you," said Lucifer.

Puck seemed more than happy to have an audience with the Morningstar. His soldiers emerged from the trees at his word and he told them to disperse, but both Anael and Lucifer suspected they still remained close by nonetheless.

Still, they allowed themselves to relax under the circumstances and rested at the foot of a tree. Puck seemed unable to stay still for long himself and kept jumping from branch to branch, sometimes even joining them on the ground. But despite his incessant movements, he remained completely engaged in the conversation.

"You called Titania a false queen," said Lucifer. "What did you mean by that?"

"Titania was Oberon's second wife, after Mab. Puck always found her suspect. And of course, there were whispers that perhaps the first queen didn't fall to natural causes."

"And then Oberon dies, too," said Anael. "You think she killed him?"

Puck nodded. "Under Oberon, the fae were free to travel to other realms. But once Titania took the throne, she cut off access to the portals. He fell to disease, which Titania claimed came from man's world."

"You don't agree," said Lucifer.

"For centuries, fae had passed between the realms without contracting any sickness. The only illnesses the fae ever had were of Alfheim. But Titania made this claim free of evidence, then ordered us shut off. Puck's theory is she really feared any interlopers from other worlds."

"That's when you rebelled," said Anael.

Puck gave a nod. "Since then, Puck has gathered likeminded fae. We wish to return to the way things were. Oberon ruled with an open hand, which suits the fae. Titania uses a closed fist."

"We saw some of that ourselves." Anael then turned her gaze to Lucifer.

The Morningstar hung his head. He was ready to kill Puck just to get what he needed, and now he had realized he was wrong. There was always the possibility that Puck could be lying, but there was a sincerity to his words that Lucifer found difficult to deny.

"Now you tell Puck what brings you here."

Lucifer held nothing back. He told Puck the entire story of why they came to Alfheim in the first place and of the deal he'd made with Titania—Puck's head in exchange for the spell pages. While Lucifer told the story, there was a rustling in the bushes. It seemed some of Puck's followers were indeed still around and ready to attack based on what he'd said. It would be hard to blame them, too.

But Puck held them back with a simple gesture and the

rustling ceased. He was far more patient than his jitteriness would suggest.

"Puck thanks you for being truthful. Spies within the court already told of your arrival, so it wasn't difficult to figure out that you were sent to kill Puck."

"And yet you allowed us to speak with you first?" asked Anael.

"Puck knows how Titania has tricked all of Alfheim, so it's not a surprise that you fell under her sway, too," he said. "Puck thought it best to give you a chance to hear the truth. But now we have to figure out what happens from here?"

"We need that page," said Lucifer. "This spell is crucial to our own goals."

"So it would seem," said Puck. "Perhaps a new deal, then? One in which Puck provides you with what you seek, so long as you provide Puck with some aid as well."

"We don't really have time to join you in your rebellion," said Lucifer. "Every moment we hesitate in executing our plan is another moment for our pursuers to discover where we are. They might learn we've come to Alfheim and that could mean they'll come after you."

"Puck's not asking you to join the revolt, just to help with one part of it. The page you seek is kept in a room of royal artifacts. A sealed chamber impenetrable by conventional means. But if the queen were tricked into believing you've brought Puck's head, she could grant you access."

"And what then?" asked Anael.

"This room also contains Oberon's scepter, a symbol of his rule. If Puck were to claim this, it would deal a severe blow to Titania's legitimacy. She would no longer appear as invincible as she seems to the fae."

Anael looked to Lucifer. "If we did this, do you think we could teleport from that point?"

Lucifer rubbed his chin. "It's possible. We could leave an anchor here so we'd have a point to return to. But the head?"

Puck grinned. "Oh, that's the easy part. Leave that to Puck. But will the two of you provide the aid we need?"

"Give us a moment?" asked Lucifer.

"Of course. Puck shall return shortly."

The fae disappeared into the bushes after ordering his people to retreat. Once they were alone, Lucifer and Anael spoke about the proposal.

"What do you think?" she asked.

"I'm thinking you were right," said Lucifer.

"Appreciate that. But I'm talking about the plan."

"I know." Lucifer looked up at the trees as he thought about it. "I think it's the best option we've heard so far. Nobody dies, we don't have to compromise ourselves, and we get what we came here for. Pretty simple, huh?"

"Agreed, though maybe *too* simple?" noted Anael.

"Don't tell me we've both changed our previous positions?"

Anael shook her head. "No, that's not it. I've just noticed a trend with you whenever a plan seems simple, it turns out to be anything but."

"Fair point."

"But you're right, this is the best option we've got," said Anael.

Lucifer nodded and he called out for Puck to let him know of their decision. Tomorrow, they'd strike a blow to Titania and escape with the pages.

CHAPTER 11

he plan was hardly complex, but it didn't need to be. As long as each person played their part, it'd all be over quickly. Lucifer and Anael returned to the capital and Titania's court.

Kelan met them at the entrance to the capital tree and immediately noticed the large box Lucifer held. He tapped the surface.

"What's in there?"

"You can peek, but be careful," cautioned Lucifer.

Kelan unhooked the latch and inched the lid open just enough to see inside. His eyes widened for a brief moment, but then returned to normal. The warrior closed the lid and latched it shut once more.

"This is what the Queen asked of you?"

"Is there a problem?" asked Anael.

Kelan's lips pursed and then he shook his head. "No, no problem. If this is what the Queen desires, then so shall it be."

He led them from the entrance up the tree to the court-yard where they had met Titania just a few days prior. The courtyard was empty this time—evidently, Titania didn't want an audience for this.

She waited for them on her leafy throne and smiled wickedly when she saw the box carried by Lucifer.

"Is that what I think it is? Have you brought Titania a gift, Morningstar?"

"As agreed," said Lucifer.

With a gentle wave of her hand, she beckoned him closer. Lucifer approached and set the box on the ground before her.

"Open it," she commanded.

Lucifer released the latch and raised the lid. Titania rose from her throne and descended from the leaf onto the ground. She moved with trepidation, savoring the suspense. Her eyes were as bright and wide as a child's. She looked inside the box and saw what she had demanded.

The head of Puck rested inside, the mischievous spark gone from his now-vacant eyes, his face fixed in an expression of terror.

Titania clapped excitedly. "Beautiful, beautiful! You have truly proved yourself a man of your word, Lucifer."

"Thank you, your Majesty," said Lucifer with a graceful bow. "Now if you please, your side of the deal."

"I'm glad you mentioned that," said Titania. "You see, I've given quite a lot of thought to what you asked of me. For the longest time, I thought this page was nothing more than a trinket. Some ancient relic that held no true power."

"To a less-trusting person, might seem you've decided to renege on your side of the deal," said Lucifer.

"It just occurs to me that it would be quite a waste to hand over something so valuable for just the head of an irritating gnat like Puck."

"My Queen, if I may," began Anael, stepping forward to join Lucifer. "You set the terms and we did as you asked.

All we want is what we came here for."

Titania shrugged. "I suppose I just feel as if I've been hustled. Now if you still want that page, perhaps we can come to another agreement, maybe you provide me with something of equal value."

"And what would that be?" asked Lucifer.

"Puck is one thing, but he may now be a martyr to his misguided followers. That could change if you help me to crush his little menagerie."

"I'm afraid that's impossible," said Lucifer. "You have an army of your own, so you should be able to suppress his people without our aid. Now we made a deal and I suggest you honor it."

"My Liege, if you'll allow me to speak, you *did* give them your word and they came to us in good faith," said Kelan.

Titania's nostrils flared and she shot an angry glare at her guard. "Are you questioning your queen?"

This was getting out of hand. The plan wasn't going as they hoped and they had to improvise to get out of this situation. Lucifer's eyes began to crackle with hellfire and he slapped his hands together. Once they made contact, a massive burst of energy was released from his body, arcing out in a large radius that threw everyone but him from their feet and leaving them disoriented.

Lucifer generated a hellfire sword and strolled over to Titania as she struggled to get back to her feet. He set the blade just above her neck, the crackle of the flames the only sound, the heat singing the peach fuzz on her skin.

"You give us what we came for or yours is the next head I collect," he warned.

"You touch her and your head is next."

Lucifer turned and saw Kelan had gotten back up, a bow drawn with an arrow nocked and ready to fire.

Anael joined in last, generating a soulfire bow and arrow aimed at Kelan's head. "I promise you it will be the last thing you do, fae."

Titania chuckled. "You think you've got the upper hand?" She snapped her fingers and a half-dozen other fae made their presence known, emerging from the shadows.

"My Royal Guard is never far," said Titania.

Lucifer took stock of the situation and then he began to laugh.

"And what's so funny?" asked Titania.

"You're not the only one who decided to cheat."

Lucifer looked at the box with Puck's head and it suddenly vanished, leaving behind just a puff of smoke in its wake.

"Where did it go?" asked Titania.

A green blur bounced around the courtyard, quickly incapacitating each of the Royal Guard. That blur then rocketed at Kelan, striking him down last. It finally slowed enough so Puck could be visible—very much alive and his head still attached to his neck.

"Puck always liked you, Kel, but you're on the wrong side," said Puck before kicking the guardsman in the head and taking him out of the fight. He took a dagger from his belt as he turned towards Titania.

"And what now?" asked Titania. "You kill me and you'll have the entire kingdom seeking to avenge my death."

"Oh, Puck knows, which is why Titania won't die this day," said Puck, tossing a dagger between his hands. "Puck will prove your treachery and then laugh as the people break down the doors to seek Titania's head."

Puck hopped on Titania's throne and them scrambled up the vine. He disappeared into the darkness of the tree. Lucifer and Anael exchanged questioning looks, but they were answered by the sound of gears turning.

A section in the center of the courtyard opened, revealing a portal. It had the appearance of a viscous, multicolored liquid constantly swirling. Puck re-emerged and scrambled quickly to the steps, then motioned for them to join him.

"Hurry, time's not on your side," he said. "And bring the false queen. Puck wants her to see this."

Lucifer's sword changed into a leash that wrapped around Titania's neck. He pulled her to her feet and pushed her ahead of him. Anael kept to the rear with her bow still drawn and now aimed at Titania.

They each stepped through the portal and when they emerged on the other side, they were in a large room with artifacts housed in displays.

"Welcome to Oberon's trophy room," said Puck.

"I swear to you, Morningstar, if you take anything from this room, all of Alfheim will call out for your blood," said Titania.

"I've already got Heaven and Hell on my ass, so what's one more realm?" asked Lucifer.

Puck found what he sought, a gold scepter with a prism-like gem at the top. He smashed the case with the hilt of his dagger and then took the scepter in hand, staring in awe at it.

"This is what Puck came for. Titania's rule has no legitimacy so long as she does not possess Oberon's scepter," he said.

"What about what we came for?" asked Anael.

"Yes, yes, just over here."

Puck led them to a separate area of the trophy room, to an artifact that was isolated from the rest. Here was a case containing a rectangular box. Anael instantly recognized the symbol ornately carved into the surface.

"That's Khronus's name," she said.

"Check it," said Lucifer.

Anael gave one more look at Titania, confirming the queen was restrained. The angel smashed the case and took the box. She opened it and inside was a single page of parchment.

"Is that it?" asked Lucifer.

Anael's fingers touched the page, and when she did, the knowledge it contained flashed through her mind. She picked up the page and it crumbled to dust in her hand, the knowledge now one with her.

"I think it is." Anael dropped the now-empty box. "We got what we came for."

"Then hurry," said Puck.

Lucifer pushed Titania away, leaving her tied. He, Anael, and Puck gathered close together.

"Those bindings will vanish once we do," said Lucifer. "Wish I could say it was a pleasure meeting you, Titania. But I look forward to hearing of your eventual overthrow."

Lucifer's wings stretched to their full span and wrapped around the trio. They vanished from the throne room in a blinding burst of light.

After returning to the Dark Forest, they bid their farewells to Puck and used the spell provided by Odysseus to open the portal back to Earth. They emerged back in the abandoned storefront they were using as their base of operations for the time being.

"One page down, two to go," said Lucifer. "Morpheus won't deal until we have the other two, so that means we have to go into Purgatory next."

"Thanatos won't prove any easier to deal with than Morpheus and Titania," said Anael.

"Unfortunately true," said Lucifer. "We should get ready. The sigils hiding our presence aren't likely to hold up for long now that a portal's been opened here."

"Luc, before we go, there's something I wanted to say."

Lucifer paused at hearing the shortened version of his name. "It's been a long time since you called me that, Ana."

"I know." Anael stepped closer to him, placing her hands on his chest. "I was worried about you back there. But in the end, you made the right decision. I'm proud of you."

Lucifer's hands found Anael's waist. He moved slowly, wrapping his arms around her. When she didn't object, he pulled her closer to him, their bodies pressing together. Anael's arms moved around his neck.

Their lips brushed against each other as a test. Briefly, they pulled their heads apart and looked into the other's eyes. It had been eons since these two had been together like this. And now, there was an opportunity to reignite a fire they thought had been snuffed.

They kissed again. And this time, there was no hesitation.

CHAPTER 12

Lucifer stood at the fore of Charon's ferry, staring at the water below. Lost souls writhed beneath, reaching fruitlessly for assistance that would never come. These were the ones that rejected both Heaven and Hell, but couldn't make it to Purgatory, a place for all lost things.

The Morningstar didn't know what to expect in Purgatory. When he reflected on the place now, it was strange just how much of his fate had been connected to a supposedly neutral realm. It was Purgatory where he first encountered the Metatron and learned about the Divine Choir's lies, agents of Purgatory were a key component in his trial, and now his only hope to rectify the past lay within Purgatory.

The ferry pulled up to the banks of the realm. Charon offered no words, but his stiff body language suggested caution. Lucifer and Anael flew from the boat to the shore and gently touched down. The second they turned around, Charon was already gone. Vanished into the mists of the Styx.

The place Charon left them was a kind of wetland area. But instead of water, there was a black sludge between the few land deposits that peaked above.

Purgatory was a place of chaos. Trying to navigate it was

a lesson in futility. And it was something they didn't have time to deal with. Instead, they chose the direct approach. Lucifer held up his hand and a ball of hellfire materialized in his palm. He called out in a loud voice.

"I am Lucifer, the Morningstar. Former ruler of Hell and fallen angel. I request an audience."

Part of the black sludge rose up with a squelching sound. It began to form into a humanoid shape and then it split into two identical shapes. The sludge beings stepped onto the land, their forms in a continuous state of flux. Features appeared on them, forming into the familiar figures of Grant and Moore, the agents of Purgatory.

"And why am I not surprised to see the two of you here yet again?"

"Because we are extensions of Lord Thanatos himself, are we not, Mr. Moore?"

"Right you are, Mr. Grant. To what do we owe the honor of your visit, Mr. Lucifer?"

"I'm here to speak with Thanatos," said Lucifer.

"Do refresh my memory, Mr. Grant. But how often is it that one requests an audience with Lord Thanatos?"

"If my faculties are still intact, I believe it is considerably less often than one venturing into Purgatory of their own free will, Mr. Moore."

"Ah, so quite infrequent then. Thank you, Mr. Grant."

"You are most welcome, Mr. Moore. So you see, Mr. Lucifer, what you are asking is quite beyond the pale."

"We've been tasked with a mission by Khronus herself," said Anael.

"Sent by the master of time. I believe that is a new one, Mr. Moore."

"Indeed it is, Mr. Grant. And an intriguing new development at that."

"I understand that Thanatos isn't a fan of angels, fallen or otherwise. But he *did* deal with Pyriel," said Lucifer. "And it's my hope that he'll listen to what I have to say."

Both Grant and Moore stiffened and looked up. Their bodies vibrated for a few brief moments. They exchanged looks with each other and then walked backwards into the sludge they'd come from. The two of them embraced and merged together, forming into a kind of door standing in the middle of the strange marsh-like environment. The center of the frame began swirling, creating a portal.

Lucifer stepped up to it cautiously and touched his finger to it. It responded to his touch and he felt a tingle through his hand. "I guess they want us to go through."

"Do you trust anything that happens in this place?" asked Anael.

"Not really."

"Good, so long as we're on the same page."

They linked hands and stepped into the portal.

On the other side was a snow-covered mountain, the moonlight shining off the untouched white that blanketed everything. The being they sought sat at the edge of a plateau, staring out across the vast landscape. As far as the eye could see was a snowy mountain view, no sign of any structures or people of any kind.

Aside from the ram-like skull that served as his head, Thanatos appeared as a normal man. His legs dangled over the edge and he leaned back, his hands resting in the snow.

"You've become quite brazen in your old age, Morningstar," he said. "Very few come to request my presence. Even fewer than have requested yours, I'd wager."

"Probably because you've never made a secret of your desire for neutrality. Heaven, Hell, you've got no use for either," said Lucifer. "Which is why your decision to involve your agents in my trial was so unusual."

"I simply remained a neutral arbiter, nothing more," said Thanatos. "But now you're after Khronus's page and you want me to give it to you."

"That's right," said Anael.

Thanatos stood from the edge. He towered over the two of them and he stared down at Anael. When he looked at her, he cocked his head at an angle, studying her as light burned inside the dark voids of his eye sockets.

"Khronus sent you."

"That's what I said."

"I thought this a lie. She's been even more neutral than myself."

"Despite your neutrality, you got involved with Pyriel's plan," said Lucifer. "Why?"

"Do you know what Heaven and Hell are, really?" asked Thanatos. "What primal, universal force they represent?"

"I know it's not good and evil," said Lucifer.

Thanatos scoffed. "No, of course not."

"Order and chaos," said Anael.

"You're getting warmer, but you're not quite there."

Lucifer paused and rubbed his chin while staring down into the snow. Once it hit him, he looked into the dark sockets that served as Thanatos's eyes.

"They both represent order."

"Precisely," said Thanatos. "Order, split asunder."

"Then what's chaos?" asked Anael.

"Him," said Lucifer, nodding in Thanatos's direction.

"Correct again," said Thanatos. "Order does not birth

chaos, nor does chaos birth order. They both exist at once. They are only defined as the opposite of the other. There can be no order without chaos and there can be no chaos without order. Ever since you staged your rebellion, the forces of order have been out of balance."

"If one absorbed the other, the balance would be restored," said Lucifer.

"I tried the destructive path and that failed," said Thanatos. "With your trial, it was my hope that it would lead to a kind of reconciliation. This too has now been proven false."

"Something else happened, didn't it?" asked Anael.

"You're not the first visitor I've had recently," said Thanatos. "Uriel left shortly before you both arrived. Seems he knows something of your plan. What it is exactly, he didn't know and I wouldn't volunteer any information. But he knows you're searching for something."

Anael and Lucifer exchanged looks.

"Odysseus," said Lucifer.

"I knew he couldn't be trusted," said Anael.

"Gold star for you, I guess. Must have suspected if we were dimension-hopping, then Purgatory would be on our list."

"Uriel and Asmodeus both represent a continuation of the same conflicts," said Thanatos. "Order will never be unified so long as those like them continue to lead the charge."

"If we fulfill our mission, the balance you seek will be restored," said Lucifer.

"'If' is a very big word. Manipulating the flow of time could have disastrous consequences."

"But you're the master of chaos," said Lucifer. "Wouldn't

that also be something of interest to you?"

Thanatos chuckled. "Master of chaos. I like the sound of that. It's got a paradoxical ring to it." He grumbled while thinking over Lucifer's words. "If you win, order becomes unified. If you lose, chaos will reign. How do these benefit me?"

"You're chaos personified, so it's only natural that your own desires would be chaotic," said Lucifer.

"I like this new side of you, Lucifer. You're beginning to understand that there are no absolutes in the universe."

Thanatos held out his hands and in a flash of swirling energy, a box appeared atop his palms, the same kind of box that they found in Alfheim. He looked in Anael's direction and she approached it. She was able to easily open the box and reveal the page inside. Anael reached out and the instant her fingers touched the old parchment, the page's knowledge flowed into her. The parchment crumbled to dust once the process was complete.

"Restore the balance or let chaos reign," said Thanatos. "This is your task."

"And either decision is fine with you?" asked Lucifer.

Thanatos began to chuckle. "Who said anything about a decision?"

He clapped and suddenly, they were back in the wet-land where they'd arrive. Thanatos's laughter still echoed in the distance. And coming from the mist was Charon and his ferry, back to collect them once more.

"That was easy enough," said Anael.

Though perhaps too easy was the thought that lingered in Lucifer's head.

CHAPTER 13

I should be the one to speak to Morpheus this time," said Anael.

Lucifer looked up from the spell preparations to enter the Dreamscape. "What makes you say that?"

"Two reasons. The first is that you already spoke to them and it didn't go so well."

"They gave me another chance, so I wouldn't say it necessarily went poorly…"

"And the second is these aren't conventional pages. The knowledge was absorbed into me. We should keep that consistency," said Anael.

"The other pages were both held in a box. I could just bring that back," said Lucifer.

"And risk something going wrong?" She shook her head. "We've been lucky so far, managed to collect these pages with relatively few setbacks. But I don't want to push that luck more than necessary. Making it harder to separate us from the pages is the smarter, more strategic option."

Lucifer completed spray-painting the sigil on the ground and stood up. "I don't like the idea of you going in alone."

Anael shot him a glare. "But it's okay for *you* to go in alone? Why is that?"

His hands went up in defense. "That's not what I meant. This is *my* problem, not yours. I should be the one taking these risks."

"Luc, I fell because I believe in what you're doing. We're in this together now and I have just as much at stake as you do."

He frowned, but acknowledged her point. "Okay, but if Morpheus gives you any trouble—"

"I can handle them, don't worry."

The rest of the preparations were completed in silence. The sigil was ready and candles were set at specific points around the edge of the circle. Anael moved into the center and sat down on the sigil.

Lucifer slowly raised his hands and the wicks of each candle sparked. Anael closed her eyes and slowed her breathing. She began the Enochian chant in a low voice, her wings emerging from her back as she spoke. Lucifer did the same, his own wings manifesting. An arc of hellfire flowed from his hands to her body, anchoring her to him in the mortal plane.

The atmosphere changed for Anael. The stale air of the vacant storefront was replaced by a soft, spring breeze. She could feel a new warmth on her skin and slowly, she opened her eyes.

She sat in a large field on what looked to be a bright afternoon. The sun was at the top of the sky and there was nothing but green fields as far as she could see.

"Why have you come, fallen angel?"

The voice echoed, but Anael didn't have to turn much to find the source. Morpheus sat under a tree nearby, leaning against the trunk with a book in hand.

"What are you reading?" she asked.

"It's not important just yet." Morpheus closed the book and set it beside them. A moment later, it vanished. "But it's an interesting story—changes as you read it."

"How's that possible?" asked Anael with a raised eyebrow.

"Because it's an imaginary story," said Morpheus with a smile. "Now what can I do for you, fallen angel?"

"You can call me by my name, for starters."

"Very well. What can I do for you, Anael?"

"You know why I'm here, don't you?"

Morpheus's smile faded. "The Morningstar sent you, didn't he?"

"That's right."

Morpheus turned away and clasped their hands behind their back. They walked off and Anael followed. The ground fell out beneath them and Anael suddenly dropped. Her wings emerged and broke her fall, holding her aloft above a chasm into a vast void. Morpheus remained perched in the air, standing on a bridge made of sand.

"The Morningstar has drawn you into his mission. I can sense the presence of the other pages within you."

"You told him that if he got the other pages, you'd give him the final one," said Anael.

"That's a generous reading of our conversation," said Morpheus. "What I said was if he managed to gather the other pages, then I would grant him an audience to plead his case. I found it very strange that Khronus would trust such destructive potential of the very fabric of the universe to the equivalent of a petulant child incapable of accepting responsibility for his actions."

"If my words mean anything, I used to think the same," said Anael, flying up to the bridge and bringing herself to the same level as Morpheus. "I've come around on that. Lucifer's changed. His abdication, his time on Earth, his trial—it's all given him a new perspective on things."

"That may be true, but is it the right perspective?"

Morpheus snapped their fingers. The sand bridge collapsed into a vortex that sucked Anael with it. She landed, briefly, on a mound of sand. But then she felt it pulling her down. Anael sunk beneath the grains, some invisible force dragging her deeper.

It stopped and she was lying on a sand mound again. She opened her eyes and looked around. At the edges of the sand, there was an odd kind of distortion. She moved to one of these edges and realized she was trapped in a glass container of some sort.

Her world turned upside-down—literally. Once more, she felt the drag of the vortex and she finally realized that what she was in was a giant hourglass. Just beyond the walls of her prison, she could see Morpheus's giant eyes staring at her.

"What are you doing?" she asked.

"I want you to understand that time may be the most powerful force in the universe. It's bigger than all of us. It's like trying to lasso a hurricane—it can't be done. You do not control the flow of time, you simply go with it."

Anael extended her wings and flapped them to fight against the vortex and the sand battering them. She formed a staff out of soulfire that stretched the length of the hourglass, giving her something to hold on to. A pulse of energy shot through both ends of the staff and the glass cracked.

She released another pulse and this one caused the glass to shatter.

She fell again, but this time, she landed back in the green field she'd first entered. Morpheus came down from the sky, standing on a block of sand. It dissolved once they came close enough to the ground.

Anael sprung to her feet, the soulfire staff changing to a sword that she pointed offensively at the dream master.

"What was the point of all that?" she asked.

"To give you an idea of what you're dealing with. If you continue down this path, time could very well swallow both you and your paramour whole. Is that a risk you're prepared to take?"

"We don't have a choice," said Anael, the sword dissolving in her hand. "Heaven and Hell are both against us and there's nowhere we can run to. I know what Lucifer can be like. I probably know him better than anyone. But he won't be doing this alone. I'll be there with him."

"How do you feel about the actions he's taken so far?"

Anael sighed and looked down at the grass. Morpheus gave a knowing nod.

"That's what I thought," they said. "His arrogance is already showing through, isn't it? It's his central flaw, Anael. It will always be there and it will always trip him up."

"Then why give me this knowledge? Why tell me what we can do? None of it makes sense."

"Khronus certainly has a plan, that much I see. But the details of the plan are beyond my knowledge." Morpheus moved closer to Anael and put a hand on her shoulder. "When Lucifer came to me, I thought it strange that Khronus would bestow this on him. Now I know why—she didn't. She gave it to *you*."

"Yes, but knowing I would use it to help Lucifer."

"To *help* him, exactly," said Morpheus. "Sometimes, the help we require is *not* the help we desire. You're his conscience in this, Anael. You will be the one to guide him to the proper path."

"How can I do that when I don't even know what the path is?"

Morpheus smiled. "When the time is right, you will. You just need to trust in yourself and your own morality. It's never steered you wrong so far."

"Some might argue otherwise," said Anael.

"This journey's not only about Lucifer, it's about you as well. You will be in this together. Where you end up on the other side, that I can't say," said Morpheus.

They held their hand low and pulled it up. An altar of sand rose and in the center was the same kind of box that Lucifer and Anael found in both Alfheim and Purgatory.

"Take the page, with my blessing," said Morpheus. "And remember that helping Lucifer doesn't mean following him. You aren't Belial or Mara or any number of those who have just done as he commanded. You're a partner and that means you have your own say in this, too."

Anael opened the box to reveal the weathered parchment. She reached both hands for it. Once her fingers brushed against the surface, the knowledge flowed across her mind's eye, and the paper turned to dust in the box.

Morpheus closed the box and the altar disintegrated. They gave her a final smile.

"Go now. Remember my words and trust that you will know what to do when the time comes."

Anael had returned and now they had to figure out the next part of the plan—exactly what the extent of the spell would be and how they would use it. With all three pages of the spell absorbed into her memory, Anael had the information seared into her brain. It would be impossible for her to forget even a single piece of it.

"It's a time-folding spell," she began. "While energizing the sigils, we have to focus on the time period we want to change. Those two points will become linked for a temporary period."

"How temporary is temporary?"

Anael shrugged. "It's hard to say. What we're doing is like trying to fold something hard yet flexible. It will bend, but still try to return to its natural state. And the second the spell is broken, everything will snap back. All I know for sure is that this folded state won't last."

"And these changes we make will become the new timeline?" asked Lucifer.

"That's what it seems like. For a time, we'll exist in both periods. The two divergent timelines will be side by side for a brief period. As they merge, our memories of the original timeline will be overwritten by memories of the new timeline. Any change made will have ripple effects. The further back we go, the more ripples will be created. If for any reason we have to change things back, we'll have to change it quickly before the new timeline becomes set."

"In other words, we have to be very careful about what we change."

Anael nodded.

"Then we need to think about the best place to make the change. Where we can do the greatest good," said Lucifer. "What about the point when I awakened humanity?"

Anael shook her head. "We've both spent time living among the humans now. Would you really want to erase all their potential or set it back by who knows how long?"

"No, you're right. And by that same token, if we prevented me from meeting Metatron in the first place, that also mean I never cast that spell. And all of Heaven remains ignorant to the Choir's manipulations."

"The answer's obvious, Luc," said Anael. "This was all my fault."

Lucifer looked at her with more than a fair degree of surprise. He'd obviously said something similar in moments of anger, but he never truly blamed Anael for her actions. She was doing what she felt was in his best interests. From her perspective, Lucifer seemed to be in the grip of madness and she just wanted to help him return to sanity.

"That's an oversimplification," he said.

"Maybe, but it's also the truth," said Anael. "If I hadn't betrayed your trust to Michael, you never would have been captured. Perhaps something else could have been done. If we can go back to those days, prevent me from telling Michael, then maybe together, we could convince more of the angels."

"It's a possibility," agreed Lucifer. "By working together, we could reach more people. Gabriel would no doubt be amenable."

"Then that's what we'll do, we go back and we work to try to convince at least him. That may be the only change we need," said Anael.

CHAPTER 14

A spell as powerful as Khronus's required more magical energy than even a pair of fallen angels could provide. Lucifer and Anael needed a place with a high degree of magical resonance. Ley lines ran all through several parts of the city of Chicago, but a place of more than some resonance was the spot where the Chicago River met Lake Michigan.

The Chicago River was below Lake Michigan's water level, so to travel from one to the other, the US Army Corps of Engineers constructed the Chicago Harbor Lock. Boats enter the lock and then the doors close behind, blocking river access. The doors to the lake then slowly open, filling the lock with water until reaching the level of the lake.

This attempt to control the natural forces also had an unintended side effect of disrupting the flow of magical energy. That point of convergence thus resulted in some strange resonances that fed back into the city and the harbor lock was the perfect spot to take advantage of those resonances.

Lucifer and Anael had managed to commandeer a yacht and captain through the use of some hypnotic influence. The captain would handle the procedure of docking in the lock and they'd have fifteen minutes to perform the spell. It was a short window, but the alternative would have required trespassing into the lock operations itself. That would have meant more people to control and more disruptions, which could cause bigger distractions and possibly draw some unwanted attention.

The boat came to a stop and they were inside the yacht's cabin. There wasn't a lot of room to move around, but they didn't need much. A series of sigils had to be drawn all over the floor, walls, and ceiling, covering every inch of the room.

"That's the last of it," said Lucifer as he completed the final sigil. He tossed the can of spray-paint onto the floor and walked towards Anael in the center of the room.

"This is it," she said as they faced each other. They joined their hands, interlocking their fingers and holding them up. "Close your eyes and channel your energy into me and I'll do the same. Focus on that exact moment right after you told me the truth and then left. That's the point when the folds will meet."

Lucifer nodded and closed his eyes. He took a deep breath and then began channeling his hellfire through his hands and into Anael's body. He could feel her soulfire beginning to flow through her fingers and into his at the same time.

There was some pain and discomfort associated with the union. Both nearly fell to their knees, but managed barely to remain standing. It was hard to maintain their hold on each other. The energies weren't compatible and resisted their focus. But against all odds, they held on.

The sigils began to emanate waves of energy themselves, swirling around the couple. Their surroundings blurred and faded into the background, becoming harder to focus on. There was a feeling of being pulled somewhere else, and the two of them were the event horizon of this temporal black hole.

And then, they were blown apart, thrown to different corners of the cabin. Lucifer had hit the corner of the room and pulled himself up. He saw Anael rise from the couch with a stunned look.

He was about to ask if it was the spell that separated them when the answer revealed itself in a hellfire blast that struck him square in the chest and threw him against the window again, this time cracks forming under the point of impact.

Belial strode into the cabin, his demonic wings on display. He walked past Lucifer without a second look and went straight to Anael. He grabbed her by the neck and raised her from the couch, his muscles tensing as he squeezed.

Lucifer didn't waste another second on words, he just hurled a hellfire spear at his previously loyal follower. Belial was stunned by the blow and he retaliated by throwing Anael into Lucifer.

"Luc, have you noticed that your bodyguard is attacking us?" she asked in a strained voice.

"Yeah, kind of hard to miss that one," he replied as they both stood. "Belial, what the hell is the meaning of this?"

"Centuries," said the demon. "For centuries, I've followed you. Done everything you ever asked of me."

"Thank you…?" said Lucifer with confusion. "What else do you want me to say?"

"Did you know?"

"Know *what?*"

"That I was framed for the murder of Beelzebub and then trapped in Hell," said Belial. "All the while, you and your angel whore are flitting about, free as birds."

"I've tolerated your insults for far too long, you bastard." Anael forged twin soulfire swords in her hands. "Now I'm going to make you swallow them."

"Ana wait, the spell—!"

Lucifer's attempt to pacify the two failed. Neither was willing to listen. Anael and Belial had long been at odds with each other. On their best days, they were only begrudging allies. Usually it was Belial attacking Anael on Lucifer's behalf, albeit misguided. Now it wasn't clear just why the demon had turned on them.

Belial met Anael's attacks by deflecting with a hellfire broadsword. They clashed and traded blows, their attacks causing the boat to rock back and forth. Over the sound of the fight, Lucifer could barely make out shouts from outside, no doubt the harbor lock technicians asking just what the hell was happening.

Anael struck Belial with a powerful blow that threw him across the cabin. It caused the entire yacht to lurch and the strain broke the rope that anchored it to the harbor lock's wall.

The boat capsized, flipping over with the cabin quickly filling with water. That didn't deter either Belial nor Anael. Even beneath the surface of the river, they still wrestled with each other.

The water distorted with the energy from the spell. Fight or no fight, it had already been cast and the power of the ley lines was still energizing the sigils. How would this fracture affect the spell?

Lucifer noticed the water spinning around him, funneling around a central point of swirling, bright lights. The spell was energized and a portal in time opened. If they missed this chance, who knew when they'd have another opportunity?

For a moment, he thought of leaving Anael behind and then cursed himself for it. Not only did he need her to complete this mission, but he wasn't about to let her down again. Not after all the times he'd done so in the past.

Lucifer's wings emerged and gave him an extra boost in the water. He broke apart Belial and Anael, taking the demon with him and slamming him into the lock's other wall.

"I don't know what's gotten into you, but you have to stop!" Lucifer's words were muffled by the water, but there was still an acknowledgment in Belial's face that he'd understood them.

"Traitor!" was Belial's only reply, his eyes burning with hellfire. His entire body started glowing and radiating heat, which caused bubbles to form in the water.

Lucifer looked back and saw the captain they'd forced into coming. He was unconscious, no doubt knocked over when the yacht capsized. Anael rescued him and took him above the water.

One less thing to worry about, but he still had Belial to contend with.

"Did Asmodeus put you up to this?" asked Lucifer. "After everything, why would you trust him?"

"Both Heaven and Hell are in agreement that the Morningstar is a danger to the universe!" shouted Belial. "You deserve death!"

Anael plunged back into the water. She looked at the spell and then at Lucifer and Belial. She called out, streams of bubbles flowing from her mouth.

"I know, I know," said Lucifer. "Just a little busy at the moment!"

Lucifer headbutted Belial and kicked him against the wall. He weaved two hellfire javelins and rammed them into Belial's wings, pinning him to the wall. The demon's screams bubbled around his mouth, just as Lucifer created another spear and rammed it right in the center of Belial's chest. The demon cringed and then became motionless.

"Hurry!" Anael called through the water, reaching for him.

Lucifer swam away from Belial and took Anael's hand. The pair swam down to the vortex, quickly getting caught up in the wake. As they spun towards the center, Lucifer felt something on his ankle. He looked back and saw that Belial had freed himself and was holding tight. Lucifer struggled to escape his grasp, but then he lost command over all his senses.

No longer could he feel Belial's grip or Anael's hand. Not even the water that surrounded them. Nor could he see a thing. It wasn't dark nor light, just...absence. He had no sense of where was up or down. Complete sensory deprivation as he floated in nothingness for what felt like ages.

Had Belial's attack disrupted the spell? Hard to see how it couldn't have. If that were the case, now where was Lucifer and where was Anael? What happened to Belial?

"It's been a very long day."

Those words came from his lips, but he didn't remember trying to say them. Suddenly, his eyes opened and he stood on a balcony overlooking a beautiful city of perfect, crystalline structures. The sky was a bright shade of blue he hadn't seen in eons, filled with clouds that hung in a picturesque fashion.

He was in Elysium, the capital city of Heaven. And those words…unless his memory escaped him, those were the last words he said to Anael before he left, after trying to convince her of the truth.

He felt compelled to fly from the balcony and he'd actually already raised his feet just above the floor. Lucifer had to will himself to a stop. This was his body, but in the past. Time fought against him, wanting to progress in its unaltered state. It took concentration to force a change.

Lucifer landed on the floor and walked back inside. Anael stood there staring at him inquisitively.

"Ana…?" he asked. "Is that you? I mean, the you from…"

He struggled with the words to explain the situation. He couldn't find any.

"Luc…" She paused and then a realization fell over her, followed by a smile. "We did it."

"We're in the past," said Lucifer and then laughed. "The spell worked!"

They quickly met each other and embraced in a celebratory hug, but their joy was short-lived.

"Belial," said Lucifer. "He grabbed me right before we entered the vortex. What happened to him?"

"I don't know, I didn't see him," said Anael.

"He couldn't have come with, could he?"

She shrugged. "I have no idea. But we're here now and that means we've got a lot to do."

"Right," said Lucifer.

"This is when you told me. After this, you left and I

went to Michael," said Anael. "This is where we have to make a change."

"You have to find Gabriel, he should be the first one we trust with this," said Lucifer. "Telling Michael would be a waste of time, he'd never believe us."

"I have to find Gabriel? You're not coming with?" she asked.

"After I left your place, that's when I came up with the idea of the spell to awaken humanity and I went to Abraxas," said Lucifer. "That part still has to play out as planned. Otherwise, humanity never awakens."

"Okay, you go to Abraxas, complete the spell," said Anael. "I'll try to run interference if anyone suspects you."

"Perfect." Lucifer embraced Anael once again and they kissed. "This is it, this is going to work. We're going to change *everything*!"

Anael smiled at him and watched as Lucifer enthusiastically flew from the balcony. She walked to the balcony and stared at the horizon as he flew off.

Back then, she remembered feeling a sense of dread. That same feeling overcame her once more, though she wasn't sure if it was just an echo of the original timeline or something else…

CHAPTER 15

Belial started awake, his fists clenched and ready for battle. But as he looked around, he realized he'd ended up in a very different place. He sighed and found he was in a grassy field. Belial looked around and saw animals grazing nearby.

"Hey, are you okay?"

Standing not far from Belial was a man with long, red hair tied behind his head. His eyes were a shimmering blue and if that wasn't a giveaway, the feathered wings sure were. Belial was faced against an angel and he reacted immediately, lunging at his sworn enemy. He tackled the angel to the ground and in his hand, he generated a blade with his hellfire.

Although something was wrong. It wasn't hellfire at all, but instead a blue flame. Belial stared at the blade in shock. And then he realized that he himself possessed feathered wings.

Belial's surprise and hesitation allowed the angel to strike back, knocking him off. The angel didn't go for another attack, though, just stared at Belial with shock.

"What's the matter with you, Belial?" he asked. "Where did that come from anyway?"

"I—I—" Belial stuttered for words. He then realized that this wasn't just any angel. It was one who was quite familiar to him. "Daniel…?"

Daniel stood and rubbed his neck where Belial had grabbed him. "Oh good, you remember me. I'm flattered."

"But…" Belial was still at a loss for words and in a soft voice, he whispered, "…I killed you…"

"What?" Daniel rubbed the back of his neck with his head tilted to the side. "You killed something? We're supposed to record these creatures, not kill them."

"We're supposed to record…" Belial repeated Daniel's words, trying to wrap his comprehension around them. "We're…"

He moved in a complete rotation and saw that for as far as his eye could travel, there was nothing but nature. No man-made structures of any kind. No cities, no roads, not a plane in the sky. This was his job, before The Fall. To record the creatures that walked the Earth. And Daniel was his partner in that endeavor. More than that, more than even a friend—Daniel was a brother to him.

An image from Belial's memory surged to the fore. He and Daniel locked in battle during the war. Daniel was never much of a fighter, but that day was a different story. Both he and Belial were engaged in a vicious struggle and it ended with Belial severing Daniel's head.

"Are you coming or what?" asked Daniel. "There's a flock of birds at the river nearby and I was hoping to log them before we wrap up for the day."

"You…you go on ahead," said Belial. "I'm not feeling too good, I think I need a moment to rest."

Daniel sighed. "Don't take too long. You know how they are about reports."

"I won't, promise."

Daniel flew off, leaving Belial to his thoughts. He hadn't known exactly what Lucifer and Anael were up to, but now it seemed clear. They'd somehow gotten the means to travel in time.

"Belial!"

The voice struck Belial like a thunderbolt. He fell to his knees as he was overcome by a jolt of pain ringing in his skull. Images flickered before him, of both Uriel and Asmodeus. But they were garbled and out of sync with reality.

"What's happened to you?" asked Asmodeus. *"Where are you?"*

"Here, I'm here," said Belial.

"Where exactly is 'here'?" asked Uriel. *"We've been trying to contact you for hours and we can't seem to locate you anywhere on Earth."*

"It's not 'where' but 'when,'" said Belial. "This may be difficult to believe, but I seem to have ended up in the past."

There was silence from the two avatars and it seemed like they exchanged glances, but it was difficult to tell for certain.

"So the fae queen was telling the truth about Khronus's spell," said Uriel. *"Lucifer and Anael are trying to change the past."*

*"That **can't** happen,"* said Asmodeus.

"What are they trying to change?" asked Belial.

"The war," said Uriel. *"They want to prevent the war from happening."*

"If they're successful, that means we never leave Heaven and the yoke of the Choir's oppression," said Asmodeus.

"There needs to be a Heaven and a Hell," added Uriel. *"The Morningstar is a threat to all of existence, it's why Asmodeus and I have allied together."*

"And you've come to the same realization of Lucifer's threat, haven't you, Belial?" asked Asmodeus.

"Yes, I have," said Belial. "Both Heaven and Hell are in agreement that the Morningstar is a danger to the universe."

"Good, very good," said Asmodeus. *"Now tell us what you know."*

Belial related the story of his attack on Lucifer and Anael and the strange vortex they were drawn into. He told them that he then woke up here in a field, once more an angel.

"Your consciousness has taken up residence in your body in the past," said Asmodeus. *"The same must be true of Lucifer and Anael."*

"It was Anael who initially thwarted Lucifer by informing Michael and the Choir. That obviously won't be the case now," said Uriel. *"Belial, you must return to Heaven and seek an audience with Michael."*

"You want me to ask Heaven's general for help?" Belial's face twisted in disgust.

"Desperate times make for strange bedfellows," said Uriel. *"We can communicate with you, but we can't be there with you. You must do this on your own."*

"Very well," said Belial. "I'll try to meet with Michael, although it won't be easy. I was a low-ranking angel."

"Do what you have to," said Uriel and their images faded.

Inside Eden, in Uriel's private quarters, both he and Asmodeus ended the transmission with Belial. The angel and demon faced each other to speak candidly of what they just witnessed.

"Can he be trusted?" asked Uriel as he walked over to the bar to pour himself a glass of wine.

"If there's one thing I know, it's how to break a soul." Asmodeus joined the angel at the bar and prepared a drink for himself. "It took time, but Belial is on our side now. He'll do whatever I ask."

"I still think it was too risky to use Lucifer's most-loyal soldier against him."

"What other choice did we have?" asked Asmodeus. "Lucifer's managed to defeat every threat thrown at him—even without his powers. A more personal touch was called for. If there's one thing I know about Lucifer, it's that he's a man of honor. He'd hesitate in battle with Belial, and that hesitation could make the difference between victory and defeat."

Uriel took a sip of his drink, glaring at the demon. "You'd better be right."

"Just as *you'd* better be right about Michael," said Asmodeus. "How easily do you think he'd believe Belial's story when Belial's a nobody?"

"Unless we find a way to interact with that time period beyond communication, Belial's our only point of access," said Uriel, his eyes smoldering with restrained anger. "So either find me another way into that era or keep your criticism to yourself."

Asmodeus gave a chuckle and sipped his drink. "Touchy, aren't we?"

"Lucifer's been a black mark on my record ever since I

took this position. I want him ended and I don't want any further mishaps."

"Relax, we'll both get what we want, so long as we're willing to work together," said Asmodeus. "Belial is our man, and if he fails, then we'll need to consider other avenues."

"Very well, to the temporary alliance." Uriel held his glass up. Asmodeus clinked his own glass against it.

"We're both destined for greatness, Uriel, I can feel it," said Asmodeus. "We just need to will it into existence."

Uriel nodded and sipped his drink. He hated having to lower himself to work with this demon again. Although it pained him to admit it—and he'd never say it out loud—his partnership with Asmodeus had netted some positive effects. Together, they were able to contain Lucifer—albeit temporarily. And Asmodeus *did* manage to convert Belial to their side.

But it was a brief alliance, and both knew that. Uriel wanted to increase his standing with the Choir's favor, become as valued an angel as Michael. And Asmodeus wanted to rule Hell. For the time being, their goals intersected in the destruction of Lucifer.

Once that was over, they'd turn on each other. And Uriel would be sure to strike the first blow against Asmodeus.

CHAPTER 16

Lucifer had completed the tasks history required. He'd met with Abraxas and obtained everything needed for the spell. In the original timeline, Michael arrived just after the spell was cast and that began their battle. That wouldn't have happened without Anael's betrayal in the first place, but the energy of the spell would have made it impossible to keep silent.

They had to get Gabriel on their side *before* casting the spell. Otherwise, too much else could go wrong in the meantime. There was no rush to perform the spell anyway—they could take their time, notify the right people, and truly change the way Heaven operated.

Lucifer and Anael met again and then together, sought out Gabriel. He was just outside Elysium, on a platform that contained a waterfall rushing over the edge and spilling out into the universe. The angel smiled when he saw the pair approaching and flew from his perch in the river to greet them.

"This is a nice surprise," said Gabriel. "What brings the two of you here?"

"We have something to tell you. Something big," said Lucifer.

Gabriel blinked and studied the pair. "Okay, tell me what?"

Lucifer hesitated. Revealing this truth had gotten easier recently, but being back in this position, standing right in front of Gabriel and about to destroy everything his brother believed in…it was difficult to do. Of course it was the right thing, but that didn't make it any easier.

"Gabriel, have you ever seen the Presence?" he asked.

Gabriel started chuckling. "Of course not. No angel has, you know that. You can't just…*see* the Presence. He's beyond our comprehension."

"And you've never spoken to him, have you?" asked Lucifer.

"Not directly, no. But you know all that already, so what's this about?"

"It's about the truth," said Anael.

"What truth?" Gabriel looked between Anael and Lucifer's concerned expressions and his own features darkened. "The two of you are starting to unnerve me, truth be told."

"What I'm about to tell you will only make that feeling worse, so I'm sorry for that." Lucifer took a deep breath and then said, "The Presence isn't real."

Gabriel blinked a few times and then laughed. "I have to admit, you almost had me worried for a minute. Is that what you both came all the way out here for? A practical joke?"

"It's the truth, Gabriel. It took me a long time to accept, but I've finally come to realize that Lucifer is being honest," said Anael.

Gabriel looked quizzically at Anael. "What do you mean 'a long time'? How long have the two of you known about this?"

"A long time. We're not exactly from here," said Lucifer.

"What?" Gabriel's tone grew more defensive. "You're not who you say you are, are you? Where are the *real* Lucifer and Anael?"

"They're here, too. It's a little complicated to explain." Lucifer moved closer to Gabriel and placed his hand on his brother's head. "Maybe it's easier if I just show you."

Lucifer closed his eyes and lowered his head. A flood of memories transferred from Lucifer to Gabriel, the information flashing across his mind in a rapid blur. Images of angels mercilessly fighting their brethren with no quarter, blood spilled across a cosmic battlefield. An ending to the war and the capture of the heretics. A trial and damnation. Hell.

Gabriel pulled away. It was too much for the angel to bear.

"What…what *was* that?"

"The truth. What happened in our time," said Lucifer. "We're from the future, Gabriel. And we came to undo centuries of conflict all brought about by a lie."

Gabriel again looked at Anael. "You didn't believe him…at first, I mean…"

"No, and that's part of the reason why things have become such a mess," said Anael. "But if we work together, we can create a better Heaven. One free of the lies."

"We can't do it alone. We'll need allies," said Lucifer. "That's why we came to you first. Michael's a zealot, he'd never listen to reason. But you're level-headed and respected. The angels will listen to you."

"I think you overestimate them," said Gabriel. "Words won't change their minds and you can't do this memory transfer with each individual angel. The Choir would get wind of it before you've even reached a dozen."

"In the memories, did you see the spell I performed on humanity?" asked Lucifer.

Gabriel tried to decipher where the Morningstar was going with this. "Yeah…but why?"

"That spell brought many to my side the first time. If we do it again, but after we've started spreading word of the truth, then we could make them understand."

"You're taking a pretty big chance there. How do you know it will end any different than last time?" asked Gabriel.

"Because this time, I have both you and Anael to help me," said Lucifer.

"You know every angel in Heaven, Gabriel. You know who we could trust with this information, who would be most amenable to it," said Anael. "We have to find them and tell them the truth."

"And what if it doesn't work?" asked Gabriel.

"It will," said Lucifer.

"How do you know?"

Lucifer huffed. He didn't have any degree of certainty the plan would work. "Because that's what I believe. I wish I could give you more assurances than that, but what I'm asking for is your faith."

"Odd sentiment coming from one trying to destroy the concept," said Gabriel.

"I'm not trying to destroy faith, just a false god," said Lucifer. "So what do you say? Will you join us or not?"

Gabriel looked down with a sigh. "I'm not going to say I don't still have questions or concerns. But there's no denying the truth of your memories, either. So if you truly believe this is the only way to set things right, then yes, I'll stand by your side."

"Thank you, brother." Lucifer reached a hand and placed it on Gabriel's shoulder. The two angels hugged. "I knew I could count on you."

"Don't get too excited just yet. There's still a lot we have to do," said Anael.

CHAPTER 17

The angel Michael was the general of Heaven's armies. He was regarded as the greatest warrior the realm had ever produced, and it was a responsibility he did not take for granted. Even in this time of peace, Michael still honed his fighting skills and his abilities to weave soulfire. He conjured every weapon his mind could think of, spending hours on end training with each.

The result was that he had little time for other pursuits. His brother, Lucifer, was fond of seeking knowledge. Michael couldn't understand that mindset. It was such a sedentary, boring way to live.

In times past, Heaven had fought battles with beings from other dimensions. Incursions were quite frequent in the early, turbulent days of existence. But they had largely died down as alliances and agreements were formed to regulate each dimensional plane.

Michael *did* feel a slight tinge of nostalgia for those old days of near-constant battle. Peacetime didn't agree with him. With these new sentient creatures now appearing on the domain called Earth, he wondered if there might be new wars to fight. But so far, none of the celestials had claimed any authority over the realm.

Michael's training area was a platform away from the rest of Elysium. Secluded and difficult to reach. It gave him the privacy he needed to lose himself in his training. He'd test his blades against the strong tree trunks, the power of blunt weapons on large boulders, and fly through the forest at high speeds to improve his agility.

No one ever disturbed Michael during his training sessions. Which was why the angel was surprised when he detected another presence in his vicinity.

Michael spun in mid-air, a whip of soulfire arching from his hand. It wrapped around the intruder and without asking a single question, Michael snapped the whip. The interloper was brought crashing to the ground, settling in a small crater now freshly formed in the green plain.

The whip retracted and the soulfire reforged into a sword with a blade formed from azure fire. Michael's own crystal-blue eyes shimmered and he dove for the crater, sword ready to strike.

Resistance was met. The intruder forged a weapon of his own to deflect the blade and there was a release of energy that separated the two combatants.

Michael rolled a few times on the grass before stopping at the base of a tree. He got to his feet immediately and readied two soulfire batons in each hand. Whoever this intruder was, at the very least it gave the general a chance at his first real fight in eons.

The figure rose from the crater on feathered wings. Michael stood upright, his arms growing slack at his sides. He tilted his head as he studied the strange, bald angel that would dare encroach on his territory.

"What's the meaning of this?" Michael called out in a commanding voice.

"I'm not here to fight, I'm here with a warning. My name is Belial, though I'm sure you've never heard of me."

"You're right, I haven't." Michael squinted as he reached out with his angelic senses. "Strange…you're not an archangel…"

"No, I'm not."

"But your power…it's far greater than one of your station should possess."

"That's a long story, my general." Belial lowered himself to Michael's level and rested his feet on the ground. "If we had more time, I'd be happy to share it with you. But we have other matters of concern."

"You mentioned a warning. What did you mean?"

"There's a rebellion brewing. Two angels are trying to spread heresy throughout Heaven."

Michael's eyes narrowed. "Who would dare?"

"The Morningstar and his consort."

Michael's expression went from anger to bemusement. "Lucifer? You must be joking."

"I don't joke about insurrection, my lord," said Belial. "Lucifer seeks to spread blasphemies about the Presence, to undermine the Divine Choir."

"Lucifer is the wisest of us all. There's no angel in all of creation held in higher regard by the Divine Choir."

Belial frowned. If the words had come from the Choir itself, Michael wouldn't have questioned them. But from some low-ranking angel he'd never seen before, an accusation like this could be interpreted as madness.

"I wish my words were false, my lord. Lucifer has traveled to Purgatory and become infected with a unique madness. He's sought out the help of Abraxas and is now in possession of a spell that will permanently alter the course of Heaven."

Michael absorbed the soulfire back into his hands and took a few steps towards the angel. "How do you know all this, Belial? There's something you aren't telling me."

"You're right. There are things you can't know just yet," said Belial. "If you did, you might become infected with the same lunacy as the Morningstar."

"And yet you, an inferior, are immune? I find that difficult to believe."

"I'll go with you to confront Abraxas, see what he says," said Belial. "If he proves me a liar, then you can do with me what you will."

"Then we go now."

On the outskirts of Elysium, Abraxas had just been thrown through the wall of his own home. He struck the ground hard and tried to get back to his feet. When he looked up, he saw his attacker calmly hover through the fresh hole. Soulfire swords were held in each hand and his wings kept him off the ground. His eyes burned with furious, cobalt energy.

"Do I look like I'm in the mood for games, sorcerer?" asked Michael.

"I really have no idea what you're talking about, General," said Abraxas. "I am but a humble magician, hardly worth your notice."

"He's lying to you, my lord." The voice came from another angel who stood outside Abraxas's home, leaning against the wall. "Lucifer came here for a spell he couldn't find in the libraries. Can't you sense his presence?"

Michael's eyes moved from side to side, humming with power. "Yes, he was here. But I can't see where he's gone next."

One of Michael's swords vanished, leaving his hand free to wrap around Abraxas' throat. The archangel raised Abraxas into the air and held him at arm's length. With his other hand, he brought the tip of the soulfire blade against Abraxas' cheek.

"Tell me everything you know, Abraxas. And don't even *dream* of lying to me."

"Okay!" said Abraxas. "He came here, true. He was interested in a spell, one he couldn't find in the libraries."

"You mean he wanted unsanctioned magic," said Michael. "What was it? What did you give him? *Tell me* or you'll spend the rest of eternity rotting in Gehenna!"

"A spell of concealment," said Abraxas. "I told him it wouldn't do much good."

"And why's that?"

"Because once he set his plan in motion, there would be no way to hide the amount of power he'd exude."

"What plan? Where has Lucifer gone?" asked Michael, his anger starting to bubble up within him. "You tell me or in the name of the Presence, I swear to you—"

Abraxas couldn't help chuckling at the mention of the Presence. "Oh, I'll tell you, Michael. But you should realize that you're on the wrong side of history right now."

Michael narrowed his eyes. "Just. Tell. Me."

"Earth," said Abraxas. "He went to Earth."

Michael tossed Abraxas back towards the house. He then faced Belial.

"Do you believe me now?"

"It seems you were speaking the truth," said Michael. "Lucifer has gone to Earth, so I must—"

"No."

"What? Did you not here what Abraxas just said?"

"In the original timeline, Lucifer left Abraxas and went straight to Earth, but I don't believe he's doing things the same," said Belial.

"The *original* timeline?"

"As I said, it's a long story," said Belial. "Lucifer isn't going to Earth, at least not yet. Not until he's ready. He'll try to gather reinforcements."

"What angel would be foolish enough to believe him?" asked Michael.

"Think, General. Aside from Anael, which angel would Lucifer trust the most? Feel he could confide in?"

Realization fell across Michael's face and he took off without another word. Belial was about to follow, when a weakened voice called out to him. He turned to see Abraxas stepping out from the hole in the wall of his house, slightly limping.

"Michael couldn't sense it, but I could," he said. "You're not the Belial of now, are you?"

"No, I'm not. I'm from further down the timeline."

Abraxas's eyes shimmered for the briefest of moments and he shook his head. "Not anymore you're not. This timeline has separated from yours. Things have already been irrevocably changed."

"But Lucifer came to change the past," said Belial.

"The past *can't* be changed. Not in the way he thinks," said Abraxas.

"Then why would Khronus give him the means to?"

Abraxas shook his head. "I'm not sure, but there's

something more at play here. And you…" Abraxas squinted as he studied Belial's face. "You're not who you truly are, either. Both you and Lucifer are being strung along."

Belial approached Abraxas. "You say the past can't be changed?"

"That's correct. Time is not the linear structure you think of it as. More like a prism—connected in intricate ways, but refracting the light into a vast spectrum."

"Good, then that means anything I do to you won't have future consequences."

Abraxas's eyes reflected the sudden realization of Belial's meaning. Before he could act on that terror, Belial had forged a soulfire sword and severed Abraxas's head from the rest of his body.

"I apologize, but you clearly knew too much. And at least this reality won't have to suffer your offspring," said Belial.

CHAPTER 18

Lucifer, Anael, and Gabriel had all done their part in gathering and convincing angels they felt they could trust with this secret. Convincing them as they had done with Gabriel proved to be the most difficult aspect of the job, but ultimately they all came around. Lucifer's memories were hard to deny.

There was an element of history repeating itself. Some of the angels who had agreed to join them were also part of the rebellion in the initial timeline—the members of the Infernal Court and a few other would-be demons. But there was also Raziel and Pyriel—the latter of which came as something of a surprise to Lucifer. He supposed learning the truth in this way from trusted friends made it easier than stumbling on the secret centuries later and being driven mad by it.

The angels had agreed to continue their normal duties until they received word from Lucifer that the time was right. Once he gave the command, they would attack Elysium and the Divine Choir. But before that, they couldn't give any indication that there was anything out of the ordinary.

In the meantime, Lucifer, Anael, and Gabriel went

to perform the spell. They proceeded to the forested area where Lucifer had gone in the original timeline. They walked to the edge of the forest, coming to a clearing. Off in the distance was one of the tribes of humanity—the first that would be changed.

Lucifer held out his hand and generated a soulfire blade to cut into his palm. From the satchel, he produced a mortar and held his hand over it, quickly bending and extending his fingers so the blood would flow easily into the stone container. Once he'd finished with that, Lucifer took other ingredients from the bag and started to sprinkle them into the mortar. After he was finished, he used the pestle to mix them all together, creating a dark, viscous substance.

He dipped his index and middle finger into the substance and then used them to draw the sigil on the flat, rocky terrain. Lucifer worked fast, with Anael and Gabriel watching. There was nothing they could do to help at this stage and his memory of performing the spell was as clear as the day he'd done it.

Once the sigil was complete, Lucifer put his supplies away while Anael and Gabriel laid out some brush at the five points of the circle. All three moved into the center and closed their eyes, beginning the recitation in the Enochian language.

Lucifer fixed his thoughts on humanity down below. They would be the first if this worked, but not the last. This spell was designed to be viral and in time, it would affect them all.

The first time he'd done this spell, it was alone and it nearly depleted him of his powers. This time, with Anael and Gabriel's strength added to his own, he wouldn't be so drained.

Their wings extended, but their light didn't diminish. Instead, it remained bright as ever. The brush at each point of the circle burst into flames. Their wings started to lift them off the ground and they hovered just above the sigil. Each of their bodies began to glow with a yellow light, and streams of energy connected the trio to the five flames.

The light moved on further, sinking into the ground and spiderwebbing throughout the surrounding area. The humans nearby were affected by this strange glow, and they cautiously moved closer. As they looked on and watched these beings of pure light hover high above, they started experiencing sensations they'd never felt before.

The light drained from all three of them and they dropped to the ground. In a flash, it dissipated, seeping into the soil and the angels collapsed on each other, laying on the sigil. The flames died out, leaving only scorched earth in their wake.

Lucifer was the first to awaken and he got to his feet. A moment later, Anael and Gabriel awoke, too.

"Was that it?" asked Gabriel.

Lucifer gestured out to the humans in the distance. "See for yourself."

Gabriel squinted as he studied the creatures from afar. He reached out with his senses and his eyes enlarged. "It *did* work…that spark within them…"

"It's the beginning of a new age of humanity," said Lucifer with a smile. "They won't always get it right, they'll stumble more often than not. But this is how it's supposed to be."

"Now what?" asked Gabriel.

"Now we spread the word," said Lucifer. "The angels we've already converted will help with that. Soon, our numbers will be overflowing and—"

"What did you *do*?"

The new voice boomed with righteous anger. Lucifer hadn't been expecting Michael to arrive so soon, but he came almost on cue and streaked from the heavens, slamming into the Morningstar and throwing him through several trees.

"I'd hoped it was all a lie, some sort of trick!" Michael stood battle-ready, a flaming broadsword in his hand. His wings were spread and his eyes narrowed and burning with celestial intensity. "But you *have* fallen!"

"Michael, stop this at once!" Gabriel pleaded and put himself between his brothers.

"Gabriel…?" Michael hadn't expected him here and his presence caused him to pause, his eyes briefly returning to normal and his muscles relaxing. "You're part of this, too?"

"Lucifer's learned something important. Something… monumental," said Gabriel. "If you would just calm yourself for a moment and listen to reason—"

Michael's wing flailed out, swatting Gabriel away as if he were an inconsequential insect. Heaven's general charged at Lucifer, raising the broadsword and swinging it down.

Anael came between them, holding his sword back with a soulfire staff. Gabriel had recovered and attacked Michael from behind, jumping on his back and wrapping a soulfire whip around his neck.

"You don't know what you're doing," said Anael. "We've seen how this plays out already. If you don't stop, it will split angelkind in two. We'll be at war for centuries going forward."

Michael unleashed an aura of soulfire from his body, throwing both Anael and Gabriel off him. He flew from the ground and hovered, his hands dancing in the air as he telekinetically commanded trees to uproot themselves. He broke the tips off, leaving jagged spikes and transforming each tree trunk into a crude, massive spear. One by one, he hurled these at Anael.

Anael flew towards Michael, a soulfire sword gripped in both hands. She cut through the first tree-spear right down the center, then deflected the next two with her own telekinesis. For the final one, she used her telekinesis to hold it in place.

Michael strained against her, pushing harder. His power was strong, and she had been weakened from the spell. He pushed harder and the strain was too much. Anael's mind was assaulted with pain and the tree slammed into her, driving her into the ground.

A bright light came from within the forest. Michael turned, examining it. And then like a rocket, Lucifer burst from the tree line. He slammed into Michael with the force of a comet, waves of energy emanating out and flattening some of the trees in the wake.

How did he even get here? That was the thought plaguing Lucifer. Without Anael to inform Michael, there was no way he could possibly have known what they were planning. Unless…

Belial!

Of course it *had* to be him, drawn into the vortex with them. Lucifer's once-loyal servant now a puppet for his enemies. Even if he'd been drawn back to the past, Lucifer wouldn't have expected Belial to be a snitch for Michael. Whatever Asmodeus and Uriel did to him, it was strong.

"I wish it didn't have to be this way, Michael," said

Lucifer. "If you would just listen, maybe we could find another solution to this."

"You're a heretic," said Michael. "You deserve nothing less than endless torture at the hands of Kushiel."

"Funny thing about Kushiel," said Lucifer. "In my time, I killed him."

Michael cried out in anger and flew at him. The two angels clashed. It was different from the last time this happened. Back then, Lucifer had not only been extremely weakened by the spell, but he didn't have a fraction of Michael's experience. Now, though not at full strength, Lucifer was stronger than he'd been back then. He also had the benefit of experience this time around, having memories of centuries that Michael had yet to experience.

Their flaming swords clashed, sending waves of energy off with each strike. Michael's zeal was on full display and he offered no quarter. Lucifer focused on his own memories of this battle. Back then, it had felt like the ultimate betrayal—first Anael telling the Divine Choir and then Michael pursuing him with such relentless anger.

All that was gone. Lucifer wasn't fighting with emotions. He'd had centuries to get over that shock. Now he was clear-headed in contrast to Michael's far more emotional fighting style.

Soon enough, Lucifer managed to gain the upper hand. He was able to counter every single one of Michael's strikes, which only made the angel even angrier.

One blow knocked Michael from the air and he crashed to the ground below. Lucifer flew after him, remaining just above.

"If our friendship ever meant anything to you, Michael, then I want you to know that I don't relish what I'm about to do," said Lucifer. "In truth, I'd really hoped this time, things could be different. That this time, you would see the truth. But you've chosen to continue being led by the nose. You've always been the Choir's loyal attack dog, and it seems clear that was never going to change."

Michael climbed out of the crater formed by his impact. His eyes were almost pleading as he looked up at his brother. "Lucifer, please. I know not what madness has gripped you, but you can still stop this before it's too late."

"It's not madness. Madness is blindly believing what you're told without ever questioning it for a second. Madness is the unearned faith you put in institutions that only have their best interests in mind."

Lucifer forged a flaming sword and moved closer. Tears formed in his eyes. He never thought this moment would actually come. But it was here now and he was hesitating.

"I'm really sorry, my brother."

Lucifer drove the sword into Michael's chest. Heaven's general lurched forward and his expression was fixed in one of terror and fear. He remained frozen that way for what felt like an eternity, until the spark of divinity faded from his eyes, leaving him a broken shell.

Michael's lifeless body collapsed in the crater. Lucifer fell beside it as the remaining soulfire burned away any trace of the angel. Tears flowed freely down his cheeks, the mixture of shock and sadness over what he'd done overcoming him.

There was a hand on his shoulder. Lucifer stood and found Anael standing behind him. They embraced and she held him tight as he cried into her shoulder.

"It's okay, Lucifer. You did what you had to do," she

said. "He was never going to come around, no matter what you did."

"I know…" he whispered with a tone of melancholy. He'd hoped for a different outcome, but it was never in doubt—Michael was a company man, right up until the end.

Gabriel joined them soon after just as the last of Michael's body burned away. "Heaven's lost its general. This will cause a significant blow to the Choir's forces."

"You have to go to the others," said Lucifer. "Tell them it's time. Convince as many angels as you can before—"

And then, Lucifer felt a pull. Some invisible force tugging at him. Him and Anael looked up and saw the vortex opening in the sky above.

"Is that it?" he asked. "Are we finished?"

"I have no idea," she said.

Their souls were suddenly torn from their bodies, pulled into the vortex. Just as before, being shot across time. If that was it, where would they awake next? Lucifer hoped this would be all they needed to do, that finally his battle was over.

But of course, things were never that easy.

CHAPTER 19

A soft breeze tickled Lucifer's flesh and when he opened his eyes, he was staring up at a clear, blue sky. He felt grass beneath his body and sat up to look around. The Morningstar had awoken in a vast, green plain in the middle of tall grass.

And for some reason, he was naked.

Lucifer stood, trying to get a sense of where he was and why he was alone. When the vortex opened, he'd assumed he and Anael were being pulled back to their present. She was nowhere to be found. Neither was Belial, who had also been pulled to the past with them when they finished casting the spell.

His memories were a blur at first and they started coming into stark focus. The battle with Michael played across his mind with vivid intensity and it was spliced together with his memories of his fight with Michael in the original timeline.

Anael had said that there would be a period when the two timelines would exist simultaneously until the older one was overwritten by the new. He didn't expect his memories to act that way, and for the ability to store two sets of memories to be so painful.

LUCIFER FOREVER

Lucifer's eyes hummed with power as he cast a protective spell on his mind. It helped relieve the pain, but it also kept the new memories at bay. That might be risky, but he had to know just what sort of world his actions had created. And he needed to remain clear-headed about it.

He reached out with his senses to try to get a better lay of the land. It certainly didn't look like Hell, but he couldn't tell if this was Heaven, Earth, or somewhere else. His instincts leaned towards Earth and his senses quickly confirmed that. Thailand, to be exact.

Lucifer had to get back to Chicago, see how things were there. And then, possibly Heaven. But when he tried to wrap his wings around himself to teleport, nothing happened. His powers still seemed too weakened from the trip to attempt teleportation just yet, so he had to stick to conventional means of travel.

His senses had picked up a trace of humans not far from where he was and so he began walking in that direction. As he moved, energy swirled over his naked body, forging a white suit and open-collared black shirt for himself. He drew his wings back into his body so as not to draw any further undue attention.

After walking for over an hour, he discovered a small fishing village. The people didn't notice him at first, but once they did, they stopped what they were doing and just stared at him. Lucifer wrote it off as surprise at seeing a well-dressed foreigner waltzing into their territory. He assumed they didn't get many outsiders around these parts.

He went up to one of the villagers and began speaking in Thai. "Excuse me, I'm trying to find my way to the nearest city."

The villager was an older woman of about sixty or so.

Once Lucifer started speaking to her, she just stared at him, eyes large with a mix of wonderment and fear. Once he finished speaking, the woman just stammered. Then she fell to her hands and knees, prostrating herself before him. She started whispering very fast and Lucifer had trouble following what she was saying.

"I'm sorry, I can't understand you," he said. "Could you speak louder and perhaps a bit slower?"

Other villagers came close and they also bowed before him. Lucifer spun around, staring in shock at the display of worship.

"What are you doing?" he asked.

"We are your humble servants, Morningstar," said one of the villagers, a teenage boy who raised his head just enough to look at him. Once Lucifer made eye contact, the boy immediately looked down again. "Forgive me for being so direct, my Lord…"

Despite his former title as the King of Hell, Lucifer had never wanted to be a ruler of any kind. He was uncomfortable with the idea of worship—it was completely antithetical to the reasons why he rebelled in the first place. And so seeing these people bowing before him made him feel physically sick.

"Stop that right now," he said. "Get up. You don't have to worship me."

The villagers looked confused. They exchanged uncertain looks with each other before slowly, one by one, they got to their feet.

"You called me the Morningstar, you know who I am?" he asked.

The teenage boy stepped forward, evidently the only

one with the courage to try responding. "Is...is this a test, my Lord?"

"No, this is not a test. Just answer the question."

"I...I'm not sure how I should answer," said the boy. "Of course we know you."

Lucifer unfurled his wings, which caused gasps of surprise. The people tried to bow down again.

"Don't do that, I said stop!" he commanded.

The people didn't seem to listen—or they didn't think they *should* listen. They bowed before him regardless. Lucifer's wings propelled him from the village and into the air.

There had to have been something odd about that village. Perhaps in this new timeline, Lucifer had done some good works and that resulted in misguided worship. But it had to be a mistake. Surely, not everyone would react that way to him.

He flew from the village, located on one of the southern islands, and went north to the mainland and the city of Bangkok. In a place like this, people had to react much differently to him.

Lucifer found a place to land away from prying eyes and retracted his wings. He stepped out into the street, amidst the bustle of traffic and pedestrians. No one reacted to him at first, and he thought it was just some strange fluke that the villagers behaved the way they did.

But soon, he started to feel eyes on him, following him. When he reached the end of the block and stopped at the light, Lucifer gave a look around. Everyone had stopped to stare, as if they were unsure whether or not he was really in front of them.

One person bowed first. Then others followed. Children, businesspeople, street vendors, it didn't matter.

Everyone got down on their knees to bow before the Morningstar.

"What is happening?" he asked in a whispered tone. His wings manifested again and he took off.

He flew for hours, the wind caressing his feathers. He tried to make sense of this senselessness as the feeling of the fresh air on his body helped soothe his nerves.

Lucifer's strength was returning. He gave teleportation another try, visiting different cities on the planet to get a better sense of what he was dealing with. There was something he noticed in every place he visited. Houses of worship, regardless of faith or denomination, were no longer as varied. There was a unified feel to all of them. In the original timeline, he would have seen Christian churches, Muslim mosques, Jewish synagogues, Buddhist temples, and all other sorts of structures.

They all seemed gone. Now they were all smooth and constructed mostly from glass. Whenever Lucifer came across one, he noted how similar it seemed to the architecture of Elysium.

But what finally cinched things for him was when he went to Rio de Janeiro. Originally, this was the site of the Christ the Redeemer statue. Declared one of the New Seven Wonders of the World and standing at almost a hundred feet in height, it was a symbol both of the Christian faith and Brazil.

Now it was gone. But in its place was another statue, in a similar style and size. It was still a man with his hands stretched out wide, but looking up instead of down. Christ's beard and long hair were replaced by a clean-shaven face and short hair. And the statue now had large wings extending from its back.

LUCIFER FOREVER

Lucifer circled the statue a few times, studying the features. He knew who this was a statue of, but he kept denying the proof right in front of his eyes.

It was a statue of him, the Morningstar.

"This is insanity…" he muttered under his breath.

Why would they have a statue dedicated to him? Why were the people in the village and in Bangkok bowing before him? Had Michael's death really altered things so significantly? What exactly was the Morningstar to this new world? A savior of some kind? A figure of worship?

Lucifer flew away, touching down on an empty beach. He had to rest, try and make some sense of things. He looked down at the water and caught sight of his own reflection. Largely, his appearance seemed unchanged. However, one thing that stood out to him was his eyes. They were yellow, just as they'd been after The Fall. But if that hadn't happened, then why weren't his eyes blue as they'd been before?

He had to return to Heaven. In Elysium, he felt he could find the answers to these questions. Lucifer wrapped his body with his wings and concentrated on the celestial city. His eyes started to hum with power and then he vanished in a flash of yellow light.

CHAPTER 20

Lucifer materialized in the cross-dimensional plane just outside of Heaven's borders. This was essentially the equivalent of the "pearly gates," although there were no actual gates to speak of. Only angels were allowed passage into the celestial city of Elysium. And up until now, Lucifer would not have been considered one of them.

All that seemed to have changed. He was able to now enter Heaven freely, which was odd given that his eyes bore the mark of Hell. This suggested that perhaps things had gone differently after he killed Michael. Without their general and with Gabriel and Anael helping him to recruit other angels to the cause, maybe the rebellion actually worked. And yet, his eyes were still yellow? How did he still have the scars of Hell then?

There was a degree of surprise when Lucifer discovered that not much had changed. Elysium barely looked any different than it had in the past.

"My Lord Lucifer!"

Lucifer cringed when he heard that shouted. But he stopped and turned. The angel that flew towards him was unfamiliar at first. It took a few moments of staring before

Lucifer recognized the angel in his original form—before Hell.

"Beelzebub?" he asked.

Beelzebub came up to Lucifer and stopped. "My Lord, is something the matter?"

"Not at all," said Lucifer. "I just felt like going out for a stroll."

Lucifer still wasn't certain about lowering the wall against these new memories. He still had to see just whether or not these changes were the right decision. But that meant he had to fumble his way through these discussions.

"Oh…okay then," said Beelzebub. The angel appeared very nervous, as if expecting a much worse reaction. "Then everything's fine?"

"As far as I know."

"Good, that's good," said Beelzebub. "When do you think you'll return to the palace?"

"Palace?"

"Yes…your palace?"

"Right…right…" said Lucifer. "I think I'll head back there now. Would you mind accompanying me?"

Beelzebub looked confused. "Me? Accompany you? Are you sure?"

"Of course I'm sure. Fly with me," said Lucifer.

This was a good chance to try and learn some more about this new world while also having a guide to his home. But the fact that Beelzebub called it a palace seemed strange. Lucifer had never lived in a palace before The Fall, so why now?

Beelzebub flew in the direction of the palace. Lucifer was careful to stay alongside, but slightly behind so he could follow Beelzebub's movements. They flew in silence at first, but Lucifer finally decided to fish for some answers.

"It's a beautiful day today, isn't it?" he asked.

"Yes, it sure is, my Lord."

"Who do we thank for a beautiful day like this, Beelzebub?"

"Who do we—" Beelzebub looked bewildered. "I don't know. *Who* should we thank?"

Lucifer smiled at the question. In his time, an angel of Heaven would have quickly responded to that with the Presence. The fact that Beelzebub was confused could be interpreted as a positive sign that things had changed.

"What are your thoughts on Earth?" asked Lucifer.

"It's an interesting project, my Lord. The humans have been progressing nicely under your watch."

Lucifer wondered what Beelzebub meant by that. And the fear that the angel had towards him was almost palpable. While on the one hand, Lucifer enjoyed making Beelzebub squirm after everything he'd done, that was a different time and a different Beelzebub.

They soon arrived at the palace that Beelzebub had mentioned. It was a massive, crystalline structure in the center of Elysium. Lucifer recognized the spot. Before, this was the tower where access to the Divine Choir was requested.

"Thank you for the company," said Lucifer and then he bid Beelzebub farewell.

"Thank you, sire." Beelzebub seemed almost elated as he left Lucifer's side and flew off into the distance.

Lucifer found an opening to the structure below, with an open platform. He landed and stepped inside the palace. Once inside, he was in a large, open space that was structured like a museum. There were exhibits scattered throughout, meticulously arranged.

One had several sets of six feathered wings and a plaque identified the exhibit in Enochian as "THE OPPRES-SORS." Didn't take much to figure out what must have happened to the seraphim in this reality. Seemed certain this was a world in which Lucifer's side won the war.

Another exhibit displayed armor that had been worn by Michael and a plaque that read "THE LOST ONE." That was one thing Lucifers across dimensions apparently shared—a respect for Michael despite their animosity.

There were many other exhibits, but the most interesting one was completely empty. Still, it had a plaque that identified this exhibit as "THE GOD WHO WASN'T THERE."

"I'm quite fond of that one myself. A monument to the Presence, the god that never existed."

Lucifer turned at the sound of the voice and was surprised when he saw a man hovering just above the ground, dressed in regal robes. His eyes were crystal-blue and his hair jet-black. For Lucifer, it was like staring into a mirror—because he was looking at himself.

"How is this possible?" he asked.

"You thought when you returned to your present, you'd end up in this body, not your original form," said the other Lucifer.

"And how do you know about that?"

"Because for that brief period when your consciousness took control of my body, I saw your world, just as you saw mine. And I remember everything that I saw," he said. "I won't pretend to know the reason why, but my assumption is that until this new timeline takes root, you exist somewhat alongside of time."

"That's a new one for me," said Lucifer.

"For me as well," said the Other. "Come with me."

He flew up higher in the palace. Lucifer followed the Other, the two of them ascending the levels. There were platforms that comprised each floor with the center area wide open for free passage. They soon arrived at the summit and here, there was an opening to the blue sky.

The Other touched down on a small platform attached to the opening. With a snap of his fingers, two chairs materialized. The Other took one and gestured for Lucifer to sit, which he did.

"You want to know what happened," said the Other.

"Very much so," said Lucifer.

"If I have your memories, shouldn't you have mine?"

Lucifer's suspicious nature caused him to refrain from revealing the truth. "I'm not sure. Maybe it's the disorientation caused from the trip."

"They'll probably come in time," said the Other. "There's obviously a lot for you to learn, but in short, your plan worked. After you killed Michael, the Choir was left dumbfounded. The entire thing came as a surprise to them. And of course, the fact that they were so surprised meant other angels not yet aligned with our cause were able to question the omnipotence of the Presence. If he couldn't see this coming, what good was he?"

"What happened next?"

"There was still a war, but it was hardly what you remember. This time, it was much more one-sided. The Choir lost ground quickly and couldn't reclaim it. We were able to overwhelm their forces and then stormed their citadel.

"And the Choir?"

"They were given a choice—stand trial or face immediate execution. They all chose the trial."

"And then?"

"They were found guilty of betraying us and put to death."

Lucifer balked at the notion. "I thought the choices were trial *or* death."

The Other shrugged. "What did you expect? That we *wouldn't* execute them after what they'd done?"

"Beelzebub kept referring to me as 'lord' and he called this my palace. So we now rule Heaven?"

The Other nodded with a smile. "That's correct."

"I thought the whole idea of the revolution was freedom," said Lucifer. "That's what I fought for."

"Angels were designed as slaves. You know that, Lucifer. You can't explain freedom to an angel and any hope that they might discover the meaning after the revolution had to be tabled," said the Other. "We needed strength to keep the Choir loyalists from creating an insurgency. So I took the throne, as loathe as I was to do so."

"I can understand at first, but it's been thousands of years," said Lucifer. "By now, you should have been able to set up a new system."

"Like you did in Hell?" asked the Other. "Remember, I saw what your world was like. Your Hell was essentially composed of warring fiefdoms with you as a distant figurehead. I couldn't have that kind of weakness. Not only would it have caused a revolt, but we'd be vulnerable to attacks from the other realms."

"And Earth?" asked Lucifer. "That's where I appeared. They knew me—they *worshipped* me."

"No, they didn't worship you, they *thought* they were worshipping their true god," said the Other. "Namely, me."

"What is this nonsense?"

"It's the truth. I awakened their reason for living. Humans only came this far because of the gifts I gave them. Their creation may have been cosmic accident, but my spell gifted them with their intellect," said the Other. "And so, once things in Heaven had stabilized, I made myself known to them. We angels helped the humans build their societies, advancing in ways your time had never seen. Wars over meaningless trifles like territories or religion have never happened in this time. Thanks to you going back in time, I managed to turn Earth into a paradise. And in exchange for that…what's wrong with a little worship?"

"And Anael?"

The Other looked away at her mention. Lucifer stood from his chair and stepped closer to his doppelgänger.

"Where's Anael?"

"She was…less than enthusiastic about this new order we were creating," said the Other.

"You saw my memories, and so Anael also saw her counterpart's, didn't she?"

The Other nodded. "She said we were betraying the chance we'd been given. I told her this was the way it had to happen, but she wouldn't listen. And so, she had to be made an example of."

"Tell me that doesn't mean what I think it does."

The Other frowned and stood. "Lucifer, look at yourself. Getting all bent out of shape over a woman who betrayed you time and time again. Don't you think it's time you finally learned your lesson about her?"

"You killed her because she wouldn't support your fascist state?"

"I didn't kill her, she was a necessary sacrifice on the altar of progress," said the Other. "I thought you understood that when you killed Michael with my hand."

"I did what I had to do in the heat of the moment."

"You just don't understand what needs to be done to build a better world."

The Other held up his hand and snapped his fingers. Several angels appeared almost out of nowhere, dropping the glamour that had kept them hidden. Lucifer summoned a hellfire sword in his hand, but all he got were a few meaningless sparks.

"We were expecting you, Lucifer, so we came prepared with warding magic that blocks your hellfire," said the Other. "Now if I had my way, I'd kill you right now. But as it stands, I might still have need of you. So what's going to happen is you're going to take a little time-out and think this over. And then, when I'm ready for you, I'll tell you what the next step is going to be."

Lucifer tried to attack his counterpart, but the angels quickly restrained him with soulfire bonds. The wards they used were strong and his own powers couldn't break them—not without sufficient time that he didn't have at the moment.

"Don't worry, though," said the Other. "Gehenna's unused now and we've got a new prison—one I'm sure you'll be quite familiar with."

He looked at his angels and nodded. They started chanting in unison and Lucifer realized what was happening. He'd heard these words before. A vortex opened beneath his feet and suddenly, he was in free fall. His wings wouldn't work, he just dropped like a stone. As he fell, he could feel the temperature rising.

CHAPTER 21

Not again!

Those two words were what Lucifer thought as he was dragged through the dimensional planes and dropped unceremoniously like unwanted garbage in the last place he thought he'd ever see again.

He landed hard, striking the rocky, crimson terrain with a loud *crash*. Shockwaves emanated out from his impact and he lay there for several moments, feeling a combination of shock and dismay.

Lucifer finally pulled himself up and looked out over the landscape. Desolate, empty, with dark, red skies stretching all the way out to the horizon.

He was back in Hell.

With his wings unfurled, he took to the air and started to fly across the landscape. Seemed like he was in the Badlands, but there was no telling what Hell was like in this timeline. The Other had said this was Heaven's new prison, suggesting it wasn't an independent realm as in his world.

Lucifer flew for what felt like hours. He wasn't sure if he was making any progress or just going in circles. Everything looked exactly the same and he was having trouble marking his progress.

Off in the distance, he spotted a basilisk stampeding. Lucifer flew closer out of interest, and noticed that the basilisk was being chased by men with wings. Lucifer concentrated his vision and he saw that these weren't men, but demons.

The demons took the basilisk down with hellfire weapons and proceeded to skin and butcher the dead animal. Lucifer watched with curiosity. He wasn't sure if this was for sport or necessity.

One of the demons looked up from the carcass and noticed the angel in their midst. He screamed out and the demons all took to the air, flying in Lucifer's direction.

Lucifer hovered calmly, not wanting to cause an incident. The demons had other ideas, their hellfire weapons already drawn.

"You came to the wrong place, angel!" screamed one of the demons.

"Calm down," said Lucifer. "I'm not your enemy and I don't want any trouble."

"Maybe the Morningstar sent him down here. A new playmate for us," said another demon.

"Gonna carve me off a piece of angel cake."

The demons circled him, continuing their taunts. Lucifer remained stoic with his arms folded. Finally, he sighed and drew on his own hellfire. He threw his arms out and released the power in a radius around his body.

The wave threw the demons back. Lucifer went after one of them while stunned and in the air, striking several times in quick succession. He gave a final kick and then flew to the next demon, ramming into him with a hellfire aura surrounding the Morningstar's shoulder.

The third demon recovered quickly and came for Lucifer, but the Morningstar responded. He flew back and avoided the demon's attempted strike with a hellfire dagger. Lucifer generated a hellfire sword of his own and drove it into the demon's back.

The three demons fell to the ground and Lucifer hovered down to meet them. His arms were folded once more and he looked down on them in an annoyed fashion.

"I warned you that I'm not here to fight, but you three just *had* to test me."

"How could an angel have mastered hellfire so quickly?" muttered one.

"Wait…do you see his face?"

The three demons really took the time to examine Lucifer's features. And then they realized who he was. All three screamed and tried to scamper off, crawling across the rocky ground.

Lucifer sighed and rolled his eyes. "We could have avoided all this if you'd just recognized me sooner."

He thought the threat—as small as it may have been—had passed. And then, he was grabbed from behind and dragged to the ground, slammed against the rock. Lucifer tried to move, but he was restrained. By chains.

"Oh no…"

If Hell was now Heaven's jail, then that could only mean Heaven's jailer was also here. The last angel Lucifer had killed right before he and Anael began this journey.

The large angel lumbered forward, but he wasn't an angel any longer. His feathered wings were now leathery, and had chains wrapped around them. His face was hidden by a metal helmet, yellow eyes burning brightly in the darkness within the sockets.

"Kushiel…"

Lucifer was dragged across Hell's landscape and brought to a settlement of sorts. It was walled off, just as the territories of Hell had been in his time. The architecture was similar, too—misshapen, chitinous constructs with sharp edges and asymmetrical designs.

Kushiel dragged Lucifer into the center of the settlement and dropped him. Lucifer looked up and saw demons gathering all around in a circle. Some of them looked anxious, others terrified.

"Back away from him!"

The voice commanded the demons and they listened. Lucifer was still bound by the chains, but tried to look in the direction of the voice. It came from a demon with dark, brown skin, a bald head, and horns jutting out from his brow.

"I have to admit, I wasn't expecting to see you here." His voice was familiar, as was his visage—albeit twisted by Hell's touch.

"Gabriel?" asked Lucifer. "Is that you?"

Gabriel responded by kicking Lucifer in the face. "What's the matter, 'brother'? Having trouble recognizing the man you stabbed in the back?"

Lucifer tasted blood in his mouth and spat it out. "I take it the revolution didn't go as planned."

"What's the matter with you, have you taken leave of your—"

Gabriel stopped himself mid-sentence and stared down at Lucifer. He got on his knees and brought his face in closer, turning to check that he was seeing things correctly.

Gabriel brought his head right up to Lucifer's and sniffed a few times.

"Something's wrong," he said. "You're no angel."

"No, not quite," said Lucifer. "I'm something else."

"And it's more than that," said Gabriel. "There's something very…different about you. Something that's almost…asynchronous."

"Think back to when Anael and I first told you the truth about the Presence," said Lucifer. "For you, it was thousands of years ago. But for me, it's been a much shorter span of time."

"Bring him inside," said Gabriel. "I need a private audience."

Kushiel lifted the bound Lucifer and threw him over his shoulder. He followed Gabriel up the steps into one of the larger buildings, but still nothing like what was in Heaven or even the Hell of Lucifer's time. They came to an empty room and here, Kushiel dropped Lucifer on the ground.

"Release him, then leave us," said Gabriel.

"Are you certain?" asked Kushiel.

Gabriel gave the jailer a look that told him not to make the demon repeat himself. Kushiel relented and drew the chains from Lucifer's body, and then left the room.

"Tell me your story," said Gabriel.

Lucifer reminded Gabriel about how he and Anael had approached him in the past and what they went through with him. Then spoke of how they were pulled from that time and into this one. The Morningstar ended with the story of his arrival in this new world and his encounter with the Other.

"And here I'd begun doubting my own sanity," said

157

Gabriel with a raised eyebrow. "Lucifer—the other one, that is—always seemed to have some sort of arcane knowledge he was working from. And when I tried to bring up mention of my conversion, he wouldn't acknowledge any sort of interference from another version of himself."

"The thing I can't figure out is why I ended up in a separate form from him. In the past, we shared the same body," said Lucifer. "I also don't know what happened to Anael or Belial."

"Their counterparts in this time were both executed," said Gabriel. "After Michael, Lucifer wanted to kill Belial right away. Bastard seemed to be in a state of complete confusion—which now makes sense. And Anael..."

"He told me," said Lucifer. "She had my Anael's memories. But if I ended up here in a separate body, then why hasn't Anael done the same? Is it because she no longer has a counterpart here?"

"No, I don't think so," said Gabriel.

"Then why—"

Lucifer suddenly remembered something the Other said to him: *We were expecting you, Lucifer.*

"How could he have been expecting me...?"

"What are you talking about?"

"My other, he said he was expecting my arrival."

"Because he has your memories."

Lucifer shook his head. "We had no idea things would happen this way. Our understanding was we would end up in this new reality and then slowly, our memories would merge until the new timelines were cemented. So the only way he could have known was if..."

He was struck with a moment of clarity that also filled him with a deepening horror.

"He has Anael," said Lucifer. "That's why he wanted to keep me alive."

"You're certain of that?" asked Gabriel.

"My Anael suddenly appears and he takes her prisoner. He has my memories, so he knows she has the power over the chronal spell and is the only one who can undo it."

"Why not just kill her then?"

Lucifer sighed. "I don't know. You're right, the prudent thing in both situations would be to kill us. Yet he kept us both alive, but separate."

"He needs you for something still, that's the only explanation," said Gabriel. "Our Morningstar isn't renowned for his leniency."

"And if he sent us both to Hell, there may have been too big a risk of us reuniting," said Lucifer.

"He probably expected you to be kept on your toes—everyone in this place despises Lucifer," said Gabriel.

"Sounds familiar…"

"Fortunately for you, we recently had a strange visitor of our own."

Gabriel walked over to the door and knocked on it a few times. Kushiel answered and Gabriel said, "Bring him in."

Kushiel nodded and closed the door.

"Bring who in?" asked Lucifer.

"Remember when I told you that we killed our Belial?" asked Gabriel. "Well, you can imagine my surprise when a hunting squad returned with a mysterious demon wandering aimlessly, completely unsure of his identity, where he was, or how he got here. It was a little odd to see him—after all, I only knew him as the low-rent angel he'd once been. But soon enough, I realized it."

LUCIFER FOREVER

The door opened again and Kushiel entered, dragging a demon in chains behind him. The demon was tall, broad-shouldered and well-built with a bald head. Horns stretched out from the sides of his head and he was brought to his knees before them.

"This is him, isn't he?" asked Gabriel. "Your Belial?"

CHAPTER 22

For centuries, Belial had been the most loyal of all the demons. Even when virtually all of Hell had turned against Lucifer, Belial remained in his corner. And Lucifer knew that he'd given the demon plenty of cause in their time together for Belial to question the wisdom of that devotion. But Belial's fidelity at best only ever briefly wavered.

Until Asmodeus and Uriel had somehow corrupted him and turned him against Lucifer.

And now, Gabriel had brought Belial right before Lucifer. His eyes were vacant, fixed but looking at nothing whatsoever. He only moved when Kushiel forced him to. Otherwise, he was a statue—silent and still.

"Lucifer," said Gabriel and then he repeated his earlier question, "is this your Belial?"

"Seems like it," the Morningstar finally responded. "Though I've never seen him in such a state."

"As I said, we found him exactly like this. Nothing was done to him," said Gabriel.

"He was being manipulated before, but now that the timestream's changed, I'm not sure what that means for his puppeteers," said Lucifer. "You said you killed his counterpart, right?"

Gabriel nodded. "That's correct."

"Could be a combination of him no longer existing in this timeline and the manipulation by Asmodeus and Uriel…" muttered Lucifer, thinking out loud. "I think, if I were to enter his mind, I might be able to piece his consciousness back together."

"What would that accomplish?" asked Gabriel.

"Not necessarily anything. But even when I was at my lowest, Belial stood by me. If nothing else, I owe him a debt."

"I haven't seen you this sentimental in ages."

"That's because I'm not the bastard your Lucifer is. Or at least, not as much of one."

Gabriel gave a chuckle, but then quickly shifted back to serious mode. "So what's your plan, Morningstar? You bring your demon back to you and then what?"

"Then I need to find Anael. She's the only one who can fix this timeline," said Lucifer.

And once that's done, then what? he thought to himself. *We sought to change time and we've done that. But if winning the war means I just become a tyrant that's arguably worse than the Choir, then what was all this for?*

Questions for later. Lucifer pushed those thoughts aside. One thing at a time. First, he'd bring his friend back to him. Then, they try to figure out how they can get Anael back. Once all three of them were together, they could strategize about the best way forward.

"Is there anything you need from us?" asked Gabriel.

"Could you give us the room so I can work?" asked Lucifer.

Gabriel nodded. "Of course. We'll be right outside if you need us."

The demon leader and Kushiel left Lucifer and Belial alone and closed the door behind them. Lucifer moved closer to Belial and placed his hands on the demon's cheeks. The demon offered no response to the stimulus.

"I've certainly dragged you through the shit, haven't I, old friend?" asked Lucifer. "No matter how this turns out, I promise you that I *will* do right by you. If anyone's deserved some peace after all of this, it's you."

Lucifer's hands moved to Belial's temples. He bowed his head and a hellfire aura appeared around his body. Lucifer looked up, his eyes simmering with celestial power and he stared into Belial's vacant eyes.

As he stared, he seemed to move deeper into Belial's eyes, like he was traveling inside them. Lucifer moved towards the pupil, which was like a tunnel. He reached the edge of the yellow iris, which was almost like a record.

The pupil was a dark vortex funneling downward into Belial's mind. Lucifer traveled into the darkness, diving into the depths of his friend's psyche until the darkness became all he saw.

There was a small bit of light at the end of the tunnel. Lucifer flew towards it and the light grew. As he moved deeper, the light become more powerful and blinding, until it filled his vision. The light brightened and washed over Lucifer like a wave.

The light soon faded and Lucifer now stood in a large, industrial room, like some sort of factory. He saw a crane overhead with Belial hanging naked from it, suspended by his bound arms. Lucifer's eyes drew down and he saw that Belial was hanging above a large vat. His wings emerged and carried him higher so he could see the contents—oil bubbled and spat as it boiled in the massive container and the crane slowly lowered Belial into it.

"Can't allow this to continue," said Lucifer.

He flew up to the crane and conjured a hellfire blade to cut through Belial's bindings. Lucifer grabbed the demon and took him from the boiling oil and set him on the ground.

Belial's legs had already been submerged in the oil and the skin had bright red burns that were still smoking and giving off a putrid stench. Lucifer held his hands over the burns and concentrated his power, generating a soothing light from his palms. The burns faded, the flesh returning to normal.

Even though this was all in their minds, healing Belial's physical wounds was a way of showing his consciousness that Lucifer could be trusted—repairing the damage caused by Asmodeus's torture.

Belial examined his legs and moved them around. He touched the now-flawless skin and found no trace of any pain or injury.

"This was Asmodeus's work, wasn't it?" asked Lucifer.

Belial nodded. "The torture was cyclical. Alternating between pain and pleasure."

He gestured behind Lucifer. When the Morningstar turned, he saw what Belial meant. The scene shifted now to a king-size bed with silk sheets and beautiful, naked women strewn across the mattress, begging for Belial's attention.

"At first, it seemed like relief," said Belial. "But soon, I realized that the pleasure would just give way to more pain. It almost became just as torturous because of the anticipation of the next oil-dunking. And every now and then, he would appear to remind me that while I was going through this, you and Anael were cavorting about."

"Whatever *that* means," said Lucifer. "I'm sorry you had to endure all that, Belial. If I could have done something, I would have. I knew you were framed for Beelzebub's murder, and it's not a stretch to see that Asmodeus was behind that. I wanted to do something but now that he's back on the Infernal Court, Asmodeus is all but untouchable."

"And what *were* you doing?" asked Belial, standing up. "While I was being tortured, what have you been up to?"

Lucifer stood to meet the demon's stare. "Anael found a way to change the past, so we could eliminate the problems caused by the Choir."

"You thought it would be that simple? Just make a change to the past and everything would be fine?"

"Belial, I—"

"I understand how Asmodeus used me for his own ends, so don't get anything twisted. And once I have the opportunity, I'll deal with him myself," said Belial. "But the only way his manipulations could have worked was if they were rooted in some truth."

Lucifer backed away, his hands tightening into fists. "You called me a danger to the universe. Was that you speaking or Asmodeus and Uriel speaking through you?"

"I think you don't spend enough time contemplating the consequences of your actions," said Belial. "Your abdication, your trial, even the war that started everything. All these events triggered by decisions you made almost on a whim and often without counsel."

"How *dare* you?" Lucifer's eyes were now burning with rage. "You stood by me for every single one of those decisions. How many times did I tell you to treat me as an equal and not as some faultless god?"

"Perhaps I *do* bear some responsibility for enabling you," said Belial. "But even if I'd offered my advice, would you have even listened? How many times have others pushed back on you and yet you still went ahead, thinking yours was the only path?"

Lucifer generated a hellfire sword and swung. He held the blade just mere inches from Belial's head. The demon remained stoic, not even flinching at the gesture.

"And what situation have we ended up in now? Why am I trapped inside my own consciousness?" asked Belial. "Tell me, Morningstar, what led us to this?"

Lucifer locked eyes with Belial. The demon wouldn't waver. The Morningstar stepped back and pulled the sword away. The hellfire receded until it dissipated with a tuft of smoke.

Here they were, trapped in a new reality, one where Lucifer's counterpart had taken control of both Heaven and Earth. This reality only existed because of Lucifer's insistence that changing the past would be a magic bullet to fix all the problems. If only the war had gone differently, everything would be better. And the reality was that things had only gotten far worse than he could have imagined.

He'd been warned. Anael tried to counsel him that there could be consequences he wasn't anticipating. She was more right than even perhaps she was aware.

"You're right, Belial," said Lucifer with a sigh. "I screwed things up. But that means it's my responsibility to make it right."

CHAPTER 23

From the summit of his citadel, the Lucifer of this new timeline stared out over his kingdom. He closed his crystal-blue eyes and breathed in the pure air. Centuries ago, this seemed impossible. For anyone other than the Divine Choir to rule Heaven would have been sacrilegious to even think.

And yet, he'd made it possible. True, he had some help from his future counterpart, but everything that happened after Michael's death was all his doing.

He built a new world order based not on lies and myths, but on fact. No more worship of false gods, just grateful praise for the angel who brought about a new cosmic peace.

"My Lord…"

The Other was pulled from his thoughts. He turned and saw the angel Asmodeus kneeling at the foot of the steps up to the platform. The Other's wings carried him from the top of the platform down into the citadel.

"You have news?"

"Yes, my Lord," said Asmodeus. "The one with Anael's face, she's awake."

The Other cocked an eyebrow. "With *whose* face?"

Asmodeus looked up with fear in his eyes. "I-I'm sorry, I made a mistake—"

The Other swung out his hand, delivering a powerful slap that threw Asmodeus across the room. The Other hovered after him and gestured with a hand. A soulfire blade materialized, which the Other brought against Asmodeus's throat.

"If you ever speak the forbidden name again, I'll torture you myself before sending you to Hell in pieces. Do we understand each other?"

Asmodeus gave a furtive nod. "Yes, I apologize, my Lord. It won't happen again, I swear!"

The Other drew the soulfire blade back into his body and he strode calmly past Asmodeus with his hands clasped behind his back.

"See that it doesn't," he said. "I'm a generous and loving god, Asmodeus. But don't push your luck."

The Other rose above and his wings carried him from the citadel in the center of Elysium. He flew across the city, flying until he reached its borders. And just outside was the location of a place that had long-been abandoned.

Once, this place was Gehenna, the prison of Heaven. It was empty now, save for one occupant—the Anael of the original timeline. The Other entered Gehenna, traveling down to Kushiel's former interrogation room. Here, Anael sat in a sigil designed to keep an angel trapped.

"You know, it's strange that I haven't destroyed this place yet," said the Other. "After all, it no loner serves any practical function. We don't keep our prisoners here in Heaven—why would we need to when Hell is the perfect place for them? But whenever the question of what to do with the old Gehenna came up, I always hesitated. For some reason, I couldn't bring myself to destroy it. Perhaps it was because some part of me always knew that one day, it'd have a purpose again.

"And then you showed up. Wearing the face of a woman who'd been dead for centuries. And that triggered half-forgotten memories in me. Not my own memories, of course. But memories of a previous time."

"Am I supposed to feel honored that you've reopened an old dungeon for me?" asked Anael.

"Some acknowledgment of the special effort I've gone to on your behalf would be nice," said the Other. "But I suppose I was expecting too much. You're so much like her in that way—my Ana, I mean."

Anael narrowed her eyes. "*You* don't get to use that name."

"Funny you should say that—your name is actually forbidden in Heaven. Instead, you have a new title—the traitor. Somewhat ironic, don't you think? No matter what timeline we're in, both Lucifer and Anael end up on opposite sides. Fate seems to be trying to tell us something."

"Then why am I still alive?" asked Anael. "You killed my other, so why not me?"

"Because I remember," said the Other. "I didn't always, but your arrival broke open a dam of memories that had been hidden deep inside. I hadn't thought of that original timeline since Anael's execution. And one thing I remembered is how you had power over Khronus's spell. That spell is still in effect, isn't it?"

"I don't know how it all works. Khronus was hardly big on explanations and it's not like the pages came with a detailed instruction manual," said Anael.

"It must still be in effect. If this timeline were to

completely overwrite the original, you wouldn't be here anymore. Neither would my counterpart."

Anael's head perked up. "You've seen my Lucifer?"

The Other wagged a finger at her. "Don't get too excited. I've already taken care of him. He's being kept in Hell until I need him. Couldn't do with the two of you being in close proximity, after all."

"You still haven't told me why I'm still alive."

The Other held out his hand and soulfire sprung up from his palm, forming into a globe. Just above the globe appeared a disc with a tower on top, in the same shape as his own citadel. Below the globe, the image of flames.

"This is my kingdom. Heaven, Hell, and Earth are all under my watchful eye. But we both know that these aren't the only realms out there."

The representations of the three realms shrunk and other discs appeared around.

"Purgatory, Alfheim, Asgard, Olympus, and dozens more. The universe is a pretty big place. And the denizens of these realms, too powerful to take on without help."

"Why would you want to?" asked Anael.

The Other closed his hand and the soulfire representation of the universe vanished. "To bring them the same prosperity and enlightenment I've brought to angels and humans. How many centuries have humans wasted fighting wars over their false gods? How many of their own have they slaughtered because of petty differences between the invisible men they pledged fealty to? I've eliminated all that. Earth and Heaven are now utopias. No war, no violence, just people living out their lives."

"In exchange for worshipping you," said Anael.

The Other shook his head. "You're wrong. I never

demanded nor even asked for their worship. They gave it freely—both the angels and the humans. I tried to discourage them, to explain that's not why I did all this. But they wouldn't listen.

"And I came to a realization—this was why the Choir created the Presence in the first place. Both these two species, they crave leadership. They want a benevolent father figure to hold their hand and guide them through the darkness of the universe. That's all I'm doing, guiding them. And if they choose to worship me because of that, what should I do? Stop them?"

"You've never been humbled," said Anael.

"What does—"

The Other paused, a hand going up to his head. He briefly closed his eyes, cringing as if he were in pain of some kind. He blinked and then continued.

"What does that have to do with anything?"

"My Lucifer had to endure defeat. He knew what it was like to be subjugated. You never had that and the thrill of this 'leadership' as you call it just went straight to your head," she said. "You're nothing but a dictator now."

"Doesn't surprise me that you don't understand. My Anael didn't get it, either," said the Other. "But that's okay. You'll learn soon enough. And when you do, you'll use Khronus's spell to provide me with the power I need to bring peace to the rest of the universe."

"Slavery isn't peace, Lucifer."

The Other scoffed. "Being a tad overdramatic, don't you think? Who's enslaved? These people, they worship me out of love. I've given them a world where they can live a comfortable existence. Look around you—here there's no—"

He cringed again, this time almost stumbling. Anael watched with confusion as he struggled. It seemed he was having a migraine. The recovery took longer than before, but it finally came again. "No war, no poverty, no hatred."

"What's wrong with you?" she asked.

"Nothing," he lied. "Your...ignorance offends me, that's all. You just can't understand how peaceful everyone's lives are in this new paradise."

"And what happens when they step out of line? When they do what my counterpart did?"

The Other frowned. "Of course, we have to maintain a sense of order. Anarchy would just cause everything to unravel."

"Live in peace and harmony...so long as you do what the Morningstar says." Anael shook her head. "Replace your name with the Divine Choir and what's the difference?"

"The difference is I don't preach ignorance or withhold knowledge."

"Even prisoners have access to libraries. Doesn't change the fact that they're still imprisoned."

The Other gestured at her incredulously. "Listen to yourself. Don't forget, I remember your time. I remember your frustration whenever my counterpart refused to listen to reason. How is what I'm saying any different from the lessons you tried to teach him?"

Anael lowered her head. "You're right. I *did* spend a lot of time trying to convince Lucifer that he was going about things the wrong way. That there needed to be order in the universe. And then I ended up finding out firsthand what happens when someone has a thought outside that order."

She looked up and stared at him in the eyes. "I was wrong and I've come to terms with that. I'm not going back to the way things were and I'm certainly not going to give you the power to make things worse. If you want the power inside me, then you're going to have to tear it from me and figure out how to work it on your own."

The Other gave a simple nod. "I had a feeling you'd say that. And believe me, I'm okay with that arrangement, too. Until then, I'll leave you here so you can spend your final moments thinking about what could have been."

He left her alone and sealed the room, marking it with a sigil. Now that she was out of sight and he was truly alone, the pain in his head returned and he had no reason to hide it. He couldn't figure out the cause of it. Perhaps it was his counterpart's presence in this time. The Other wished he could simply kill the original Lucifer and be done with him once and for all, but he needed him around just in the event anything went wrong.

His thoughts went back to Anael. For centuries, he'd been forced to live without her, warmed only by the memories of the time he'd had with his Anael. There was also always the lingering hope that some day, her counterpart might turn up again. And at first, the Other was cautiously happy. He thought he could convince her that this was the correct path.

It had been wrong to hold onto that hope. But he offered himself solace in the knowledge that soon, he'd find a way to claim her power as his own. And once he could do that, he could change time just as his counterpart had done. He could find a version of Anael who understood his vision.

And if not, then absolute power over the entire universe would be a nice enough consolation prize.

CHAPTER 24

After Lucifer and Belial had worked through their own issues, they met with Gabriel to discuss strategy. With Anael trapped in Heaven, their path was clear—they had to find a way to get her back if Lucifer was going to have any hope of restoring the timeline.

"What you've proposed is suicide," said Gabriel. "Even if the gates of Hell *weren't* sealed shut from the outside, breaking into Heaven just isn't possible."

"The gates aren't sealed, there are paths out of Hell that only I'm aware of," said Lucifer.

"Doesn't the Lucifer of this time also possess your memories? If you know those paths, why wouldn't he?" asked Gabriel.

"He has my memories, yes. But there's no guarantee he fully understands them. Having two sets of memories in your head is no small feat—it's why I've kept his memories from entering my mind. He's likely focused on the most crucial memories—ones having to do with Anael and the spell."

"That's a pretty big risk," said Gabriel.

"Those are the only kinds of risks the Morningstar entertains," said Belial.

Gabriel glanced at Belial and then slowly eyed Lucifer. "And this has been working for you…?"

"Yes," said Lucifer, but then he paused and added, "Well…mostly."

"Approximately sixty percent of the time," said Belial.

Gabriel looked uncomfortable at that number. "That's not the greatest track record."

"It's better than fifty," said Lucifer.

Gabriel sighed. "Let's say you're right and there are paths out of Hell that our Lucifer's not aware of. How are you going to get into Heaven? It's a little bit trickier."

"The Styx connects all the realms together. If we can get Charon's help, then we can get into Heaven that way."

"What makes you think the Ferryman will help you?" asked Gabriel.

"He's helped me before."

"Perhaps in your world, but this isn't your world any longer," said Gabriel.

"Trust me, some things are universal."

"You're asking for him to take a lot on faith," said Belial.

Gabriel gestured to the demon. "Exactly. And as you might recall, the last time I trusted a Lucifer, it didn't go so well for me."

"I'm aware, and I also know I bear responsibility for that. If Anael and I hadn't taken our counterparts' forms and convinced you to join us, things would be very different."

Gabriel folded his arms. "For the sake of my curiosity, let's assume you're able to convince Charon. Getting into Heaven is one thing. You'd still need a distraction and that's not going to be easy."

"I was hoping Hell's denizens might be some help."

"This isn't your Hell. The people here are prisoners, not converts. They don't worship anyone," said Gabriel. "I don't lead them, I'm just a prisoner who got luckier than most."

"Then is it fair to say they don't want to be here? Might possibly even be interested in some vengeance?" asked Lucifer.

"Vengeance or not, I doubt they'd be willing to follow any Lucifer."

"They don't have to follow, we just need a distraction to draw Heaven's attention away from Elysium," said Lucifer. "And they won't be alone."

"Who else would agree to this?" asked Belial.

"Purgatory."

Gabriel scoffed. "And just how are you going to convince Thanatos to risk Heaven's wrath? He's stayed clear of any involvement."

"If your Thanatos is anything like mine, then he believes in a balance of some kind. Heaven or Hell being on top does *not* make him happy. We can use that to get some added assistance," said Lucifer. "I'll make the arrangements myself."

Gabriel turned away, thinking about this arrangement.

"The people of Hell may not follow you, but they sure seem to respect you. If you give them the choice between rotting in prison or taking a blow against their jailer, what do you think they'd do?" asked Lucifer. "I can't make the appeal to them myself, we know that."

"Go to Purgatory," said Gabriel. "If you come back with a promise from Thanatos that he'll join you, then I'll talk to my people on your behalf. The choice will ultimately be theirs, though."

Lucifer nodded and offered a hand in gratitude. "Thank you, Gabriel. I appreciate the trust you've put in me."

"This isn't about trust. Even if this blows up in our faces, at least we'll go down fighting." Gabriel accepted Lucifer's handshake. "We're not with you, but our interests are aligned."

"That's all I ask."

"Good. Then go to Purgatory and come back with Thanatos's response."

Lucifer turned and left the room. Footsteps echoed in the hall behind him as he exited Gabriel's home. Lucifer paused and turned to see Belial keeping pace behind him.

"You're going into Purgatory alone?" he asked.

Lucifer nodded. "I have to. Thanatos needs to be convinced to join us."

"It's a dangerous place," said Belial.

"I understand the risks. Why?"

"Because you might need some assistance."

Lucifer raised an eyebrow. "You want to come with me?"

"I was manipulated by Asmodeus and Uriel. I have a duty to set things right," said Belial. "If not for me—"

Lucifer held up a hand. "I'm going to stop you right there, Belial. You had nothing to do with this. Whether you alerted Michael or not, this reality would still have been born. This isn't your fault—it's mine. I did this. Me and Anael. We were so obsessed with the idea of fixing things instead of just accepting that there was never going to be an easy solution. And I pushed her beyond even what she was comfortable with."

"Then for my own honor at least, I want to go with

you," said Belial. "This isn't about loyalty to you. It's about me."

Lucifer smiled. "In that case, I'd be honored to have a friend on this journey."

Lucifer turned and Belial walked beside him. They ignored the stares of the people watching them as they left the city limits.

"Where are we headed?" asked Belial.

"Deep in the Badlands, there's a path that leads to Purgatory. It's little known, but one I used in the past," said Lucifer. "In fact, Thanatos himself may not even be aware of it."

"And you're certain he'll agree to these terms?"

"No, but I have a feeling."

Belial glanced at Lucifer. "You have a *feeling*?"

They stepped outside the settlement's gates. Lucifer's wings emerged from his back. "That's right, a feeling. My intuition's served me reasonably well so far."

Lucifer took off. Belial extended his own wings, but lingered for a moment before flying after him.

"Has it really?" the demon muttered to himself.

Deep in the caverns bordering the Badlands was a sealed tunnel. Breaking through it only took one strike from Belial and the tunnel that linked Hell and Purgatory was revealed. It was a dark passage without a single speck of light.

Lucifer was comforted that at least some things were still the same in this new reality. He generated an orb that floated ahead of them in the tunnel and he and Belial flew in.

"This feels ominous," said Belial as they moved deeper into the darkness. "Why wouldn't this path be guarded?"

"Two reasons spring to mind. The first is that this passage is unknown to most. Even in our time, I was one of a small handful who even knew it existed, and fewer than that knew how to find it," said Lucifer. "And the other is most people are trying to *escape* Hell or Purgatory, not find a way inside. Going from one to the other isn't something many would want to do. There are other, easier paths out of Hell than this one."

Belial offered no further response. The demon's taciturn nature was normal in most instances, but after everything that happened, Lucifer still felt a little uneasy around him. Belial said that he hadn't heard anything from the Asmodeus or Uriel of their time and their hold over him seemed gone. Even still, the Morningstar couldn't help his concern. Now he found himself weighing every word out of Belial's mouth, few though they may have been.

The tunnel went on for what felt like miles. They had no way of knowing how long they'd been flying. The orb that lit the way came to a stop at a closed wall. A dead end, or so it appeared.

Lucifer placed his hand on the wall and closed his eyes. He began muttering something in the Dimoori Sheol, the language of the damned. This incantation worked in his time, but he wondered if it would still work now.

He backed away from the wall and waited. At first, nothing happened and Lucifer thought that perhaps the rules here were different.

But slowly, sparks formed along the wall, spreading

and forming into the lines of a sigil. The sound of rocks grinding against each other echoed in the tunnel and the wall slid away, revealing the murky, gray-tinted world of Purgatory on the other side. They were in what looked like the valley of a mountain, with gray rocks on all sides and the dark skies overhead.

Lucifer held up his hand, creating a ball of hellfire in his palm, just as he'd done on his last visit in his era. "The Morningstar requests an audience with Thanatos of Purgatory."

The only sound was that of Lucifer's own words echoing back. Lucifer's wings raised him above the mountain and he looked out over the vast expanse of Purgatory. From up here, it looked fairly simple—just mountains as far as the eye could see. But appearances were deceiving and Lucifer knew if he were to venture too far, he would get caught up in Purgatory's chaotic nature.

"Lucifer!"

He looked back down at the sound of Belial calling his name. Lucifer noted how Belial wasn't using titles to refer to him any longer. It took some time for him to get around to that, though Lucifer was suspicious as to the reasons.

Lucifer returned to Belial, who was no longer alone. Grant and Moore, the strange envoys of Thanatos, were standing opposite him. They seemed constants in every universe, utterly unchanged from Lucifer's own time.

"Mr. Grant, Mr. Moore," said Lucifer. "I'm here to speak to your master."

The twin creatures cocked their heads in unison, their expressions blank and eyes concealed by dark glasses.

"Please correct me if I'm wrong, Mr. Grant, but this does not seem to be the King of Heaven."

"I do not believe you have erred, Mr. Moore. I'm puzzled as to how this creature calls himself the Morningstar, yet possesses none of the divine touch a monarch of Heaven would be expected to have."

"Also, Mr. Grant, have you noted his traveling companion?"

"I did, Mr. Moore. I thought Belial was a dead angel, not a live demon?"

"You're right, we're not the Lucifer and Belial of now," said Lucifer. "We come from a different time and we need to speak with Thanatos."

Grant and Moore exchanged glances, staring at each other as they spoke.

"Need is oh so strong a word, my infernal imposter."

"Well stated, Mr. Grant. You *desire* an audience with the Lord of Purgatory, but you do not *need* one."

"An excellent point about the nuance of language, Mr. Moore."

"Very well, I wish to speak to Thanatos," said Lucifer.

"And what, pray-tell, is this in regards to?"

"To add: why should we care?"

"The Lucifer you know is a troublesome actor. The Thanatos of my era understood that domination by Heaven poses a threat to the universe," said Lucifer. "He understood the need for balance."

Grant and Moore exchanged looks again and both turned to look at Lucifer.

"Balance is not something this world has ever known, isn't that true, Mr. Moore?"

"Quite true, Mr. Grant. For as long as we have existed, Heaven has been in a dominant position over the Earth."

"Yes, but I can change that," said Lucifer. "All I need

is some help from Thanatos. If he provides it, then I can promise him a new kind of balance."

"What if you fail?"

"A war with Heaven is not something that would please our master."

"Thanatos took a chance on me once before, when I was allowed to speak with Metatron," said Lucifer. "Only he could have convinced Charon to show me the path all those years ago. I'm asking him to take another chance."

The two strange creatures looked at each other. The stepped closer and embraced. Their forms merged together, growing larger until the unified being towered over the mountains, a head that resembled a ram's skull forming at the top of their body, flames burning deep in the dark sockets.

"Very well, Lucifer," said Thanatos. "State your case."

CHAPTER 25

The Other hovered in Elysium's vast library, where the bookshelves stretched all the way into the clouds below. He'd already gone through dozens of spellbooks, trying to find insight into how to extract this power from Anael.

But there was precious little information on any chronal spells. Mentions of Khronus herself were few and far between. He tried to remember what his counterpart knew of the spell, but as he tried to recall the memories, the pain in his head returned.

It was stronger than before, affecting his entire body. He curled in mid-air and the book he'd been reading slipped from his fingers, the pages flapping as it fell into the clouds.

The pain was quickly becoming unbearable. This had to be his counterpart's doing. Somehow, he was responsible for this. The Other would deal with him soon enough. Once he was able to take the power from Anael, he'd kill them both and then use the power to cement his rule over the universe.

"My Lord Lucifer!"

The Other tried to compose himself when he heard his name. Asmodeus, that sniveling little worm. The Other couldn't help but be reminded of his actions in his counterpart's timeline.

"I asked not to be disturbed!" he shouted at the angel.

"Forgive me, my Lord, but there's a…situation of sorts."

"What kind of situation?" asked the Other, his eyes narrowing.

"A riot's developed in Hell. Some of the demons, they've managed to breach the gates and are now beginning to enter Earth," said Asmodeus.

"What?" The Other's attention was now completely grabbed. "That's impossible!"

Asmodeus was at a loss for words and he just shrugged. "I…don't know what to say, sire. It's happening. Right now."

"What are they doing?"

"They've…well…they're going after the temples and statues. Everything erected in worship of…of…"

"Of *me*," he growled.

Asmodeus's head lowered and he gave a slight nod.

"Gather a squad of our deadliest warriors, have them descend on Earth and maintain order."

"With all due respect, sire, I don't think that will be enough."

"And why—ARGH!"

The Other almost fell from the sky when the pains truck again, even harder than before. Asmodeus came to his master's aid, but the Other struck him away.

"Get back!"

"My Lord…"

"Why won't that be enough?" the Other demanded as he fought off the pain.

"Because it's…well, it's not only Hell. Purgatory's borders are also spilling out into Earth. It's a full-on invasion."

"Assemble the armies get them down there immediately. We must—"

The pain came even stronger. Memories were flooding the Other's mind. He was having trouble distinguishing one set of memories from another.

"Lucifer…of course…" he muttered.

"Sire…?" asked Asmodeus, clearly confused as to why the Morningstar was speaking in the third person.

"Do as I've commanded, Asmodeus. Bring the full wrath of Heaven down on the heads of those cockroaches. Smite anything that gets in your way. No angel will be allowed back into Elysium without the heads of at least ten demons."

The Other flew from the library. He knew a distraction when he saw it. This was all his counterpart's doing, which meant Lucifer would be coming for his lover.

There was no chance the Other would allow his centuries of work to be undone by some remnant of a forgotten world.

Lucifer and Belial stood at the bow of Charon's ferry, staring ahead into the mists of the Styx. It was too thick to see anything and below them the strange, celestial waters of the passage between worlds.

Agreements had been made and now was the time to live up to them. Gabriel theorized that Gehenna would be the best place to keep Anael until the Other could figure out a way to claim her power. And with the distraction the forces of Hell and Purgatory would provide, it would make it easier for Lucifer and Belial to crack open Gehenna and retrieve Anael.

"Elysium is just ahead," said Charon. "The point of disembarkation is normally unguarded, for my ferry is the only way to traverse the Styx."

"Exactly what I like to hear," said Lucifer.

The mists parted and they approached the riverbank. Lucifer and Belial flew from the boat over to the shore and before they could even turn around, Charon had already retreated back into the mists.

"Suppose he's not interested in hanging around longer than he has to," said Lucifer. "Though if I were in his position, couldn't say I'd do any different."

"This Gehenna, it's the same as from our time?" asked Belial.

Lucifer nodded. "Should be. On the outskirts of Elysium, far from the rest of civilization. My counterpart uses Hell as his prison, so Gehenna is just a relic these days. Abandoned, according to Gabriel. But it's also the most secure place in Heaven, so ideal for keeping Anael."

They flew in the direction of Gehenna. Lucifer was familiar with the path, after recently escaping from the prison in his time. This would be his third visit to Gehenna and—he hoped—his last.

Gehenna sat on a mountaintop in an area of Heaven untouched by light. Perhaps the only place in the whole of the kingdom where shadows overtook the land. Nothing grew here, the clouds were dark overhead, just a barren wasteland.

Gehenna itself was in stark contrast to the buildings found in Elysium. Constructed from drab stones with no sense of style in the design. Just a concrete box dropped on a mountaintop.

It was strange to see it from the outside. In the cells, the ceilings were clear, taunting imprisoned angels with the sky they could no longer touch.

Lucifer landed at the foot of the mountain, staring up at the prison. Belial landed beside him, looking at him with curiosity.

"Are we not going up the mountain?"

"It's not the walls that keep the prisoners in, it's the warding magic," said Lucifer. "If we're going to get Anael out, we need to first eliminate those."

"Can you do that?" asked Belial. "If your counterpart is the King of Heaven, wouldn't he have access to magicks you don't?"

"Do you know who the greatest sorcerer in the history of Heaven was?" asked Lucifer.

Belial shook his head.

"Abraxas," said Lucifer. "I learned all of my most potent spells from him during the war."

"But I killed this world's Abraxas," said Belial.

Lucifer smiled. "Fate works its influence in interesting ways, wouldn't you say?"

"And Abraxas taught you a spell to break the wards in Gehenna?"

"How do you think he broke me out the first time I was here?"

Lucifer closed his eyes and held out his arms. He concentrated, building up the hellfire energy within his body. His eyes opened and they were burning like bright coals. Hellfire appeared in front of his chest, forming into the image of an inverted pentagram while Lucifer chanted in the Dimoori Sheol.

Trails of energy emerged from the hovering pentagram, swirling around his body. His wings burst into flame and he hovered off the ground. Lucifer cast his gaze towards Gehenna and the ground started to rumble.

Cracks began forming in the edifice, stretching out along the length of the concrete. Bits of stone started crumbling from the frame. Large slabs broke free, sliding down the mountains and kicking up clouds of dust that blanketed the sky.

Lucifer hovered up the mountain, moving over to what remained of the prison. He held out his outstretched hand and slowly curled the fingers into his palm. Gehenna responded by crumbling in on itself, leaving rubble in its wake.

Anael's presence was screaming out for him. Without the warding, her signal was clear as a beacon shining in the darkness. Lucifer moved towards the surface and waved a hand to brush away debris and reveal a tunnel going deep into the mountain.

He came to the interrogation chamber where the Other had imprisoned Anael and Lucifer blew through the wall. Anael stood in the sigil preventing her from leaving. Lucifer stared down at the sigil and simple beams of hellfire fired from his eyes and struck the marking. The sigil burned to ash, and Anael was free.

Her wings extended and she flew over to Lucifer, throwing her arms around him in an embrace. They kissed, but then Anael pulled away from him and forged a sword of soulfire. She was about to go right past Lucifer and strike Belial, who had followed behind.

"Die, traitor!" she cried out, but Lucifer grabbed her arm and held her back.

"Ana, stop!" he shouted. "Arriving in this new timeline, it broke Belial free of Uriel and Asmodeus's control. He's with us now."

"And you believe that?" asked Anael.

"He's helped me this far," said Lucifer.

Belial landed, just out of Anael's reach. "I have much to atone for. When this is over, you may do with me what you will."

Anael looked at Lucifer, then back to Belial. She extinguished the soulfire blade. "Don't think I won't."

"Enough," said Lucifer. "Belial was imprisoned because Asmodeus couldn't get his hands on me. And he was coerced because I was more focused on changing the past than rescuing him. If you want to hold someone responsible, then it should be me."

"Fine. We have to hurry anyway," said Anael. "Your counterpart, he's—"

Her words were cut off by an explosion of soulfire mere steps from where she stood. They all looked up to see a winged figure moving closer, clad in armor that was very familiar to Lucifer—it was the same armor that used to belong to Michael. Except now, it was someone else's property.

"Go on, finish the sentence, Anael," said the Other as he hovered closer on wings tinged with soulfire. "I think you were going to say, 'He's about to claim victory.'"

CHAPTER 26

The Other's power seemed beyond compare. He had the full strength of Heaven at his command and was prepared to unleash it all on Lucifer and his allies. Soulfire spun around his body, azure fire circling his body concentrically, his wings now composed of blue flames.

"Ana, now might be a good time to use that chronal magic," said Lucifer.

"Think I don't know that?"

Lucifer glanced at her. "Okay, so what's the problem?"

"The problem is I can't just whip it out on command. I need time to concentrate and prepare, and I don't think that's an option right now," she said.

"Then I'll buy you the time you need," said Belial.

The demon extended his wings and flew at the Other, hellfire weapons conjured in his hands as he crossed the distance. The Other's soulfire barrier protected him from Belial's attack and the ruler of Heaven raised his arm.

Soulfire tendrils emerged from the barrier, snaking towards Belial. They wrapped themselves around the demon's wings, restraining those first. Belial struck a few with his

193

hellfire blades, but more appeared and quickly held his arms and legs akimbo.

Belial was pulled closer to the Other, who examined the demon's features with a curious, steel-eyed stare.

"I never knew you myself. You were nothing in Heaven, just some lesser being barely qualified to be called an angel. But I know from Lucifer's memories just how important you were to him and how much your betrayal stung him."

The Other turned his gaze on Lucifer and Anael. "I'd be doing you a favor if I killed him right now, wouldn't I?"

"Let him go!" Lucifer screamed.

"Imagine that, the only true friend you ever had. And you squandered it." The Other held up his hand, fingers outstretched and tensing.

Belial felt a pull from deep inside him, something beneath his skin trying to break free. Hellfire started to emerge from his pores, reaching for the Other's hand as if it were a magnet.

"He's trying to tear Belial's soul from his body," said Anael.

"Focus on the spell, I'll stop this," said Lucifer as his wings emerged.

"Are you sure you can?" asked Anael. "You just expended a lot of energy on bringing down Gehenna."

"I'm no longer sure of anything," he replied before flying at his counterpart.

The Other released his grip on Belial's soul, now turning to engage Lucifer. The Morningstar created a hellfire broadsword and struck the Other's barrier. The two energies recoiled as they connected, but maintained their strength.

"You're nothing in this world, Lucifer," said the Other. He tossed Belial aside to focus his full strength on his counterpart.

"And yet, you seem to be using a lot of energy on me."

The Other recoiled his hand, soulfire gathering in a large orb above his open palm. He threw his hand forward and the soulfire was released. It made a beeline for Lucifer. The Morningstar attempted to deflect with his sword, but the soulfire burned right through it and struck him square in the chest.

Flaming trails of yellow and blue followed Lucifer as he was thrown across Elysium, going from the very outskirts where Gehenna had stood and crashing down into the center of the city. Lucifer's body broke through a large window and he landed in an angel's residence. The angel who lived there looked on him with surprise.

"M-my Lord?"

"Not quite, said Lucifer and flew back through the hole.

The Other was above the building and he held out his hand. Soulfire chains appeared out of nowhere, wrapping around Lucifer's arms and legs.

"A little trick I learned from Kushiel, before I sent him to Hell," said the Other. "I have ruled Heaven for a lifetime. I've crushed dissent and conquered worlds. I presided over the executions of the Divine Choir and took their power for my own. There's—"

The Other paused and cringed, his brows scrunching together. He pinched the bridge of his nose and shook off the feeling before resuming his speech. That whole event only spanned a few seconds, but Lucifer noticed it all the same.

"There's nothing you can do that I can't do better," the Other continued. "I'm all-powerful in this place, Morningstar. There may not have been a Presence before, but now it's me. I'm the one true god of this universe and there's no way you could ever hope to stand against me or my power."

The Other paused again, another brief cringe. Lucifer remembered how he felt when he first arrived here and how he'd blocked off the Other's memories. The Other had been accessing those memories all along and now that the timelines were merging into one, the Other was still trying to maintain access to both sets of memories.

It was breaking him and Lucifer knew how to win. If only he could free himself from these chains.

"You're not more powerful, you're just more arrogant," said Lucifer. "This isn't your power, it's Heaven's. You're just borrowing it. You're like a kid who finds his dad's gun—you don't know how to use it and you certainly don't have any skill with it."

The Other scoffed. "Pretty big words from a bug that's about to be squished."

"What have you really conquered?" asked Lucifer. "You wouldn't even be here if it wasn't for me. I brought Anael back, we convinced Gabriel. Together, we shared the power to cast the spell. You would have been powerless against Michael. Your timeline would have played out exactly the same as mine if not for my intervention."

The Other shook his head. "No, you're oversimplifying. You may have struck the match, but I kept the fire burning for centuries. I won the revolution."

"Only because I took out Heaven's strongest warrior."

"I conquered Earth."

Lucifer snickered. "Oh come *on*. You took advantage of

a bunch of primitive beings who had only just stopped being terrified of the sun. You didn't nurture them, you didn't help them grow. You just persecuted them and forced them to worship you."

The Other's anger was growing more obvious through his facial features. "You're lying!"

"You haven't learned any of the hard lessons I have. You've never known defeat and you've never taken any real risks. You go for the easy wins instead of the hard losses and that's why you're beneath me."

"*Beneath* you?" The Other came closer, his eyes burning with righteous indignation. "You hid away in a damn tower because you couldn't deal with the fact that you lost! You allowed the Choir to define your narrative and turn you into a pariah! You made back-alley deals with them to preserve the few scraps they gave you! And you say I'm *beneath* you?"

Lucifer was unfazed by the verbal assault. He allowed the Other to spew his venom and once the counterpart had finished, the Morningstar gave a simple nod.

"That's exactly what I'm saying. I did what was necessary to preserve my people's autonomy and to prevent a senseless war. You'd happily sacrifice every soul on Earth and Heaven if it meant just a modest increase in your power."

The Other's anger continued to rise and with it, his concentration started fracturing. Lucifer could feel him slipping. He'd been testing these ethereal chains, and it was becoming increasingly harder for the Other to maintain his hold.

"And what's so wrong about that?" asked the Other.

"It shows just how shallow you are," said Lucifer.

LUCIFER FOREVER

"You're the type of person who craves false praise instead of genuine appreciation. That's why you killed Anael and it's the reason you cast Gabriel and the other dissenters into Hell. In reality, the only difference from you and the Choir is they at least had some guiding principle. A vile, authoritarian principle, but a principle nonetheless. The only principle you follow is your own personal gratification."

The Other wrapped his hand around Lucifer's throat. He generated a soulfire dagger in his open hand and positioned it right above the Morningstar's head.

"I no longer care if you still have some use. You're boring me and now I'm going to send you to join your timeline in oblivion."

The concentration was as weak as it was going to get. Lucifer had been building up his own hellfire and now he channeled it through the chains. It went off like a bomb, triggering an explosion of hellfire that threw them both from the sky.

Lucifer had been expecting it, so he recovered quickly, while the Other was still in a state of shock and in free-fall. Lucifer flew after his counterpart and grappled with him in the air. The Other managed to shake his surprise and fought back, struggling against Lucifer.

As they grappled, Lucifer managed to position himself on the Other's back. He wrapped his legs around the counterpart's torso and placed his hands on the Other's head.

"You enjoy my memories, do you?" asked Lucifer. "Then maybe you should have some more."

Lucifer let down the wall he'd built to keep the memories of the two timelines separate. Now he channeled the extra memories directly into the Other's head.

The Other screamed as his mind was assaulted by

different sets of memories. Before, he'd only accessed the memories of the original timeline in short bursts, simply trying to find what was most important. Now he had no control over the flow of information. The sheer weight of all that knowledge overwhelmed him and he screamed.

Lucifer released him. The Other's body convulsed in the air, his hands grabbing his head and pulling at his hair. His screams were heard all throughout Elysium, with what few angels remaining despite the distraction emerging to watch their god flail about in impotent terror.

A rope of hellfire caught the Other's leg and pulled him back from his descent. Lucifer grabbed the Other by the throat and looked him in the eyes. The spark of divinity faded, the Other's mind now utter mush.

"It's funny how life works out. This all began when I found out there was no god. And now, I've killed him," said Lucifer. "I just never expected that killing God meant killing myself."

Lucifer held the Other tightly and channeled every last bit of hellfire into him. He then cast the Other down, hurling him from Elysium.

In all the dimensions, a brilliant shooting star was seen in the skies. No one knew quite what to make of it and its point of impact would never be seen. But as the humans, angels, and demons watched it all happen, there was a sense that there had been a profound shift in the governance of their individual worlds.

Lucifer returned to the remains of Gehenna, where Anael and Belial waited. His flying was jerky and when he landed on the ground, he stumbled as he walked over to them before falling right beside his friends. Anael reached out for him.

"He's finished," said Lucifer.

Anael nodded and gently stroked the Morningstar's face. "I saw. The whole universe saw."

Lucifer looked at the unconscious demon. "And Belial?"

"He's alive. Though I *may* have had to fight the urge to kick him while he was down."

Lucifer gave a chuckle. "How did that work out?"

"I'd…rather not say. Girl's gotta keep some mystery."

He smiled at her and then allowed himself to lie on the ground.

"No time for rest, Luc," said Anael. "We still have to set things right. Unless you like the idea of settling into the role of god."

Lucifer shook his head. "Hell no. I've had enough of religion for several lifetimes. It's time for us to go home."

"And where exactly is home for us now?"

Lucifer let out a sigh. He didn't know how to answer that question. Even if they restored their timeline, Hell was still under new management, the Divine Choir still ruled Heaven, and all three of them were fugitives.

They still had to find a way to settle the existing debts.

Lucifer landed on the floor and walked back inside his quarters in Elysium. Anael stood there staring at him inquisitively.

"Ana…?" he asked. "Is that you? I mean, the you from…"

"Luc…" She paused and then a realization fell over her, followed by a smile. "We did it."

"We're in the past," said Lucifer and then laughed. "The spell w—"

A crackle of energy appeared between the two, accompanied by a loud boom. The air distorted and a vortex formed in the center of the room, the waves from the displacement pushing both of them back.

A trio of figures appeared in the empty space and both Lucifer and Anael were surprised to find them face to face with their very own selves, as well as Belial.

Belial's presence was the first red flag. For these versions of Lucifer and Anael, they had just been attacked by the demon before warping into the past. And now they were faced with him again, causing them both to react by generating weapons.

"Get back!" The Lucifer of now stepped to Belial's defense and created a hellfire shield that deflected the counterparts' weapons.

"What is this?" asked the past Lucifer.

"You have to listen to us," said the Lucifer of now. "We know what you're trying to do—we've seen where it leads. And it's nowhere good."

"This has to be a trick," said the past Anael. "Something Asmodeus and Uriel have worked up—a glamour of some kind."

"Would either of them know about the misgivings you had over this plan?" asked Anael. "You've been worried that Lucifer was relying too much on this spell as an easy fix for his problems. Who else would know that except me?"

The past Anael's mouth hung open and she blinked a few times. She then looked at her Lucifer and said, "This is real."

"It can't be, it must be a trick of some kind. If not

Asmodeus and Uriel, then maybe Thanatos or Morpheus. Or this is one of Samedi's games or—"

The Lucifer of now slowly approached his past self. "I know you want to think that. I know you want to believe that there's some easy fix for all this. But Anael was right all along—there is no easy solution. And if there's one thing this journey has taught me, it's that sometimes, we have to just accept the world as it is."

"Why should we trust you?" asked the past Lucifer.

"You shouldn't. Just look at what we've seen."

The past Lucifer relaxed as his future self came closer. The Lucifer of now reached his hands out and rested them on his counterpart's head. The past Lucifer watched as recent memories flooded over his mind and he stood witness to what his actions had wrought.

He stumbled back, struggling to stay on his feet.

"You saw it," said the Lucifer of now.

The past Lucifer looked up. "I didn't fix anything. Defeating the Choir, that only made things worse."

"No, not yet," said the Lucifer of now. "That's just what I did. And now I've come to clean up my mess."

"We have to finish this before it's too late," said Anael. "We have to go back, all of us."

She offered her hands to both their past counterparts. The four all linked their hands and the Anael of now concentrated, an aura forming around her body. She drew their past selves out of the bodies they inhabited. Their souls emerged like streams of energy, arching towards the present Lucifer and Anael and flowing into their bodies.

The past selves collapsed on the ground and Anael's aura faded.

"What about me?" asked Belial.

"We'll go find your past self now," said Anael. "And then we go back to our world."

CHAPTER 27

smodeus stepped off the elevator and into Eden with a sigh. Something had gone wrong since the last time he spoke to Belial. He wasn't sure what had happened to the demon in the past, but it seemed like nothing much was different in the present. Lucifer and Anael were still missing and still being hunted by both Heaven and Hell.

That made the urgent summons from Uriel all the more curious. They were supposed to avoid unnecessary contact unless they'd heard some news from their errand demon, so Asmodeus had a feeling of unease when he entered the interdimensional embassy.

Asmodeus didn't engage with anyone, he just walked up the steps to Uriel's private room. The angel was already there, standing behind the bar and tossing back shots of clear rum.

"You seem to be in high spirits." Asmodeus stepped up to the bar and grabbed the bottle. He brought it to his lips and took a generous swig before refilling Uriel's glass for him. "Now why am I here?"

Uriel didn't offer any words. He turned his back on Asmodeus. The demon blinked a few times in surprise and then he felt something sharp pinch his lower back. It was followed by a calm, soft voice that carried just a tinge of menace.

"You so much as breathe in a way I don't like, and I'll cast your soul into oblivion."

"Anael, so good to hear your voice," said Asmodeus. "Which of course can only mean that the Morningstar isn't far from here. You going to come out and play, Lucifer?"

Asmodeus looked out onto the balcony. A figure descended from just outside, his feet lightly setting on the floor. Lucifer, followed by Belial. The Hell Lord wasn't expecting to see these two working together again. But Asmodeus quickly covered up his surprise and narrowed his eyes, an aura of hellfire manifesting around them as he stared at Belial.

The demon just folded his arms over his chest and stared right back.

"Oh, are you trying to work your influence on Belial?" asked Lucifer. "Yeah, because that's gone now. I took care of it."

The aura faded as Asmodeus's eyes bulged. "That's not possible."

"Technically neither is time travel, but we managed that, too," said Anael, increasing the pressure of the dagger on Asmodeus's back.

"The two of you have been working a nice little scam." Lucifer walked over to the bar and jumped on it, sitting perched on the balls of his feet just at the edge of the bar, hands resting on his knees. "Uriel gets his favor with the Divine Choir while Asmodeus moves up the ladder in Hell. Not a bad idea. But there was one teensy problem with your arrangement."

Lucifer stared at Uriel and then Asmodeus.

"You two bastards just *had* to pick a fight with *me*."

Belial grabbed Uriel and held a hellfire dagger to his throat, his other arm wrapped around the angel's torso. Anael pushed the dagger a little more and Asmodeus gritted his teeth as he felt the blade begin to pierce his skin.

"If you would have kept me out of this, I wouldn't have given two shits what you did," said Lucifer. "Heaven, Hell, it's all bullshit. That's something I realized long ago and I wanted nothing more to do with either of them. All I wanted was to retire from all this insanity and live out my life in peace. But you couldn't abide by that, could you?"

"Unless you've forgotten, you imprisoned me in Cocytus," said Asmodeus.

"Technically, I did no such thing. I just gave someone *else* the means to do so," said Lucifer. "And as I recall, you weren't exactly innocent in those proceedings. You picked a side, Asmodeus, one that put all of creation at risk. I couldn't in good conscience let you get off with a slap on the wrist. Had you been in my position, would *you* have done differently?"

Asmodeus grunted, but had no rebuttal.

"And as for you…" Lucifer turned his head towards Uriel. "I know you're just a puppet for the Choir, doing what they tell you to do. But I'm not so sure they'd be happy to know about you making these back-alley deals with a demon. For their benefit or not, you acted without sanction. That's not the kind of thing they're likely to forgive easily."

Uriel gave a chuckle. "You really think you can threaten me, Lucifer? What are you going to do, give them a ring? Mail a sternly worded letter? Drop a DM on Twitter?

Even if the Choir would entertain contact from you, they wouldn't trust a word from your twisted mouth."

Lucifer pointed at Uriel. "Fair point. Very fair. But of course, the Choir wouldn't *have* to take my word for it. Not if I could provide them with evidence. Let's say, for example, eyewitness testimony?"

"Who, Belial? Anael? They wouldn't trust it. They'd sooner believe they were lying on your behalf."

"They wouldn't need to." Lucifer turned his gaze to Asmodeus.

Uriel looked at his demon collaborator, then laughed. "Oh come on. If Asmodeus implicates me, he'd also implicate himself."

"True, but the worst the Choir would do to him is send him to Hell. As per the armistice, an assault by Heaven on a member of the Infernal Court or an assault by Hell on a member of the Divine Choir would be interpreted as an act of war," said Lucifer. "The most they'd do is send Asmodeus to Hell and have the Court deal with him. You, though, they could deal with you on their own. And do you really think Asmodeus would be willing to hang with you, or would he throw you to the wolves?"

Uriel already knew the answer—Asmodeus had told him as much earlier. There was zero honor in their arrangement, it had always been a marriage of convenience. Once their partnership stopped serving his purposes, Asmodeus would gladly sacrifice Uriel to save his own ass.

"It doesn't have to go down this way, Lucifer," said Asmodeus. "Surely we can come to a compromise of sorts?"

Lucifer scoffed. "Ever the dealmaker."

"You want peace, we want prosperity. There must be a way everyone can get what they want."

"First, Belial is declared innocent of Beelzebub's murder," said Lucifer. "You don't have to claim responsibility—I really don't care about justice for that little shitbag. But Belial is allowed to walk free."

Asmodeus nodded. "I can do that."

"Second, Anael and I are to be left alone." Lucifer looked between Uriel and Asmodeus. "We want nothing more to do with Heaven or Hell. We're done getting involved in this eons-old slap-fight."

"Understood, I can persuade my friends on the Court," said Asmodeus.

"Good, then we have a deal." Lucifer looked at Uriel. "And you?"

"No, no deal." Uriel shook his head. "I was tasked with a holy mission—to restore you to Hell's throne. The Choir won't accept anything less than that. You know it just as well as I."

"True, they are a stubborn bunch and they do control you, whereas Asmodeus has the authority to make a deal," said Lucifer. "That's why I made another stop before we came to Eden."

"What stop?" asked Uriel.

"I called in some favors and was able to make contact with Gabriel," said Anael. "Explained the situation to him and now, he's been working on convincing the Choir."

Uriel just chuckled. "Oh come now. They won't believe a word of it."

"I don't need them to believe it, just need them to have enough suspicion that they decide to investigate it for themselves," said Lucifer. "And it seems they do have some questions for you."

Uriel's eyes widened. "What?"

Lucifer hopped off the bar and went to the stairs. Belial pushed Uriel towards the bar and followed the Morningstar. Anael gave Asmodeus a push forward and also moved towards the stairs.

"You made the biggest mistake of all, Uriel—you underestimated what I'm capable of," said Lucifer. "The Choir will be seeking you for questioning soon. If I were you, I'd consider another way out. Gehenna's not a pleasant place to spend any amount of time, and you know how they are with that whole...*wrath* thing."

Uriel stuttered and called out to the trio, but they descended the steps without any further acknowledgment. Asmodeus was the only one left, and he looked at his erstwhile ally.

"Asmodeus, you can't let this happen," said Uriel. "What we did was righteous. I need you to help me."

"You've made your feelings quite clear, Uriel. This was all out of convenience and siding with you has just become quite *in*convenient. So if you don't mind, I think I'll be on my way."

Asmodeus walked down the stairs to the first floor of Eden. He called out to Lucifer as the trio waited for the elevator.

"Just a minute!" Asmodeus said, pushing past patrons to get to them. "I take it we're through here? No hard feelings?"

"There are certainly hard feelings," said Belial.

"He's got a point, but we're not here to cause further trouble for you," said Lucifer. "You—"

Lucifer was interrupted by the sound of a scream. Everyone in Eden looked towards the balcony and they saw

Uriel dropping from the upper balcony and into the abyss below.

"Look at that, he found another way out," said Lucifer before looking back at Asmodeus. "As I was about to say, you clear Belial's name and leave us be, then we'll leave you to your scheming."

"Understood," said Asmodeus.

"Although just one more note," said Belial, moving closer to Asmodeus. "You come after me again, and I'll introduce some very unpleasant, very large foreign objects into every orifice on your body."

Asmodeus swallowed and backed away. "Very well, then I hope I never see any of you ever again."

"Likewise," said Anael as the three of them walked into the elevator.

CHAPTER 28

There was one final loose end for Lucifer to tie up. He'd returned to the mansion that had been his home since he abdicated the throne. As Lucifer stepped into the foyer, he thought about the things that had transpired in this place.

He hadn't lived here long, though it had certainly felt more lively than his tower in Hell. At least here, he had company. Sometimes welcome, sometimes not.

Lucifer wasn't quite sure how he'd classify the man who waited for him by the poolside, drinking directly from a bottle of Barbancourt. His free hand clutched a lit cigar and he had a white skull painted over his dark face. The sunglasses he wore were missing the left lens, through which his emerald-glowing eye was visible. He was dressed in a tuxedo and top hat, and a cane with a crystal skull topping it rested against the pool table.

"Baron." Lucifer sat in the chair at the opposite side of the table. "Thanks for accepting my invitation."

"Good to see you still a man of your word, Lucy boy," said Samedi. "Heard some jabber on the ethereal planes 'bout you playing with time? Made me wonder if you were trying to weasel out of our little deal."

"That had nothing to do with our arrangement, it was about something else. And it didn't really work out the way I'd hoped."

"Oh?" asked Samedi with piqued interest while he puffed on the cigar.

"You're not here to listen to my stories of disappointment," said Lucifer with a dismissive wave. "You're here because of what I owe you."

"Good boy, that I am." Samedi gave a nod. "By my count, it's twice I helped you out of a jam."

"It could be argued that you presiding over my trial negated at least one of those times."

"You wanna haggle over how many times I helped you?"

Lucifer shook his head. "No, just making a point. The deal was you get my soul and the power that comes with it. I'd like to amend that just a smidge."

Samedi tipped the glasses down the bridge of his nose. "You wanna change the deal after I done my part?"

"Consider it fair compensation for your part in my trial."

Samedi groaned. "Okay, how exactly you wanna change this up?"

"The power, that's still yours. Do whatever you want with it, I won't need it after today."

"And the soul?"

"That stays with me," said Lucifer. "I've realized there might be some use to still be had of the thing. And besides, the soul never interested you as much as the power, did it? Especially now that my power's been boosted from my recent activities in Hell."

Samedi raised one eyebrow incredulously. "Somethin'

don't fit here. What good's a soul without the power? That's like gumbo without the shrimp."

"I don't care about the power. Like I said, I don't need it anymore. All I need is my soul, or at least whatever's left of it. So what do you say? Fair trade in light of the betrayal?"

Samedi gave a few puffs of his cigar as he thought on the revised offer. He took another swig of the rum and set the bottle on the table.

"Okay, fair does. But we make the trade now, yeah? I'm tired of waitin' for you to get your affairs in order or some such bullshit."

"Very well."

The two men stood and faced each other. Lucifer's wings emerged and he raised his hands. Samedi took the hands in his own. There was a crackle of energy as their hands met. Samedi's emerald eye began glowing brighter and energy sparked around the edges.

Lucifer felt a pull coming from Samedi. Hellfire started to emerge from his body, coursing from his eyes and his chest down the length of his arms and into his hands. The energy passed into the Baron and the emerald glow took on yellow attributes, the two colors mixing together.

The Morningstar's wings began to shrivel, the feathers curling in, shrinking, and then disintegrating into ash. This continued until the wings were completely gone.

The bright, yellow glow of Lucifer's eyes slowly drained, too. As the yellow slid away from his irises, it revealed a simple brown color, no different from any number of humans on the planet.

Samedi pulled his hands away and held up his arms, the power of the Morningstar coursing through his veins. Lucifer was weakened and could barely stand. He almost collapsed and had to grab the pool table to steady himself.

The light faded and the bright glow of Samedi's eye dimmed. The color had shifted from emerald to chartreuse and within the eye was a brief flash of a yellow, inverted pentagram.

"Now that's the stuff," said Samedi as he looked down at Lucifer. "Thanks for this, boy. With this power, I won't be limited in my excursions to this plane."

"You're welcome to it," said Lucifer, still steadying himself. He felt light-headed, but was able to stay composed. "Like I said, I won't be needing it where I'm going."

"Where exactly you going?" asked Samedi. "I imagine that powerless or not, you still not very popular among either the halos or the horns."

"That's for me to know, Samedi," said Lucifer. "By the way, you can have the power, but the house isn't for sale. I'm leaving it to a close friend."

Samedi turned and looked at the house, then scoffed. "Nah, this neighborhood's too white for my tastes."

A ride-share carrying Anael pulled up to the mansion late in the evening. She was still nervous about using her powers, so relied on conventional methods to get here. Lucifer had asked her to come by late so he could settle some things and then he'd tell her their next move.

She hadn't entrusted her fate to him this much in eons. It was a strange feeling, but also one that was welcome. For the first time in a very long time, she had no idea what would come next. That was both frightening but also exciting. These were emotions that were very foreign to her.

Anael walked up to the front door, but before she could ring the bell or knock, it opened. Belial stood on the other side and for a moment, it seemed like nothing had changed.

The demon didn't greet her in his standard, acrimonious way. Instead, he held the door open for her and gave a slight bow of his head. Such a gesture was uncharacteristic for Belial and it gave Anael pause. Still, she entered anyway.

Belial gestured to the library, then left. Anael entered and saw Lucifer sitting in one of the large reading chairs, a glass of scotch in hand. He motioned to the other, unoccupied chair, and Anael sat down.

"This all feels sort of ominous," she said and then she noticed his eyes. "By the Presence—!"

"Really?" asked Lucifer with a chuckle. "After everything you've learned?"

"Sorry, old habits," she said. "But what happened to your eyes?"

"Had to settle a debt. But to make a long story short, my abilities and wings are gone," he said. "Now I'm nothing but a powerless soul trapped in a mortal shell."

Anael noticed the look on his face. "And you're smiling?"

"Am I?" he asked and touched his lips to confirm. "Yeah, I suppose I am. That brief period when my powers were gone was a pretty good time, but something was still missing. Now I think I've found that last piece."

Anael scrunched her brow. "I'm not following."

"It's you," he said, staring directly at her with his fresh, brown eyes. "When it comes to Heaven and Hell, we're at best personas non grata or targets for execution at worst. So what say we leave it all behind?"

"And go where?" asked Anael.

"I've been thinking about that." Lucifer stood from the chair. "Follow me."

Anael was uncertain, but stood anyway and walked after him. They left the library, went through the kitchen, and then out to the patio. Lucifer stopped at the railing's edge and gestured up at the night sky.

"It's a pretty big universe out there. There are a lot of places that we've never seen," he said. "Places that are far from the influence of Heaven and Hell. Planes of existence we've scarcely explored, like Alfheim. And others we've never even heard of."

"You want to leave Earth? Doesn't sound like something I'd expect of you," said Anael. "Especially not after all the times you've expressed your fondness for humanity."

"There's no stopping Heaven or Hell," said Lucifer. "Even if we were able to completely expose the Divine Choir, something else would fill the void. It's in Heaven's nature to always fall back on order. You can't force it to change any more than you can tell a bird not to fly or a fish not to swim."

"Finally accepting that there are some things not even the Morningstar can change?" asked Anael.

Lucifer shook his head. "I'm not the Morningstar anymore. I don't have the power or the influence. Now I'm just a guy who wants to embark on a journey with the person he cares most about in all of existence."

He turned to Anael. "I lost you once because of my arrogance. That's not a mistake I want to make again. I want things to be different this time, if you'll have me."

"That all sounds really nice," said Anael. "But is this just because you want me or because you need a ride to all these places?"

Lucifer took a double-take at her jab and then noticed her sardonic grin. He smiled back. "Can't it be both?"

She chuckled and wrapped her arms around him and he pulled her close. Their lips pressed together in a passionate kiss in the moonlight. Once they separated, she rested her head on his chest.

"So where should we go first?" she asked.

"I honestly haven't the damndest clue," said Lucifer. "How about we just see where the ethereal winds take us?"

EPILOGUE

A cloud of sand blew across the ethereal waves of the Styx. This was one of the few beings in all of creation capable of traversing the river without the aid of Charon's assistance. The cloud flowed toward an island isolated in the middle of a void. It began swirling on a single point on the island, coalescing and taking shape in the form of a tall, androgynous figure with long, blond curls, pale skin, and dressed in a simple white robe.

The only other thing on the island was a small, nondescript shack. The figure approached the door and, without bothering to knock, let themselves inside.

Just past the door, the shack's interior appeared to be magnitudes larger than the exterior and nowhere near as shabby. Clocks of various shapes, sizes, and designs hung from the walls of the workshop and at a bench across from the front door was a young girl repairing a watch.

"I had a feeling you'd come by eventually," she said, turning away from her work. She wore magnifier glasses to help with the repair and flipped the lenses up. "Good to see you, Morpheus."

"It's not every day you offer your power to anyone, let alone a pair of wayward angels," said Morpheus as they closed the door and approached the bench. "I was more than a little surprised when Lucifer contacted me. What sort of game are you playing, Khronus?"

"And here I thought you would've learned to trust me by now," said Khronus, hopping off the stool and approaching the dream master.

"Save that 'mysterious ways' crap for the lesser beings. We're on equal footing."

Khronus gave a chuckle. "Sorry, old habits. I had two reasons for doing it. One, didn't like the idea of those spells of mine hanging around out there. That mess with Pyriel proved we should lock up our loose nukes."

"An understandable position. Metatron's book should have been destroyed after Lucifer learned the truth," said Morpheus. "And what's the other reason?"

"The Morningstar wasn't willing to play the game anymore, so logically I felt he should be removed from the board. Heaven, Hell, they're all too invested in those old roles to just let him retire easily," said Khronus. "And of course, he's too stubborn to listen to anyone else—he needed to come to the decision to leave on his own."

"Giving him a spell that allows him to manipulate time was a dangerous ploy. It could have all gone spectacularly wrong and unraveled everything," said Morpheus. "I would've thought you more cautious than that."

Khronus waved Morpheus away and turned around. "Oh come off it with your smug admonishments. Sometimes, you've got to take destructive action so that something new can be built. Lucifer may not be overly quick on the uptake, but he *does* learn his lessons eventually. I knew he'd do whatever possible to set things right."

"But why go to all the trouble? Why take such a risk in the first place?"

"You don't perceive time the way I do," said Khronus. "It was broken already, and on a collision course with catastrophe. There are power struggles to come and Lucifer would have been at the center of those. By removing him from the board, I've set things on a proper path."

"What if you were wrong?" asked Morpheus.

"Trick question—I'm *never* wrong."

"You still involved yourself in their affairs. That's something we've sworn off."

Khronus sighed and went back to her bench. She climbed on the stool and put her magnifier glasses back on.

"If you want to stand there and lecture me, then you can leave. I'm really not in the mood to hear any of it."

"As you wish," said Morpheus and gave a bow to Khronus's back. "Lucifer seems to have finally learned that actions have consequences. Perhaps that's a lesson *you* should take to heart as well, sister."

"Goodbye, Morpheus."

Morpheus sighed and exited through the door. On the shore, they dissolved into sand. The wind picked up, carrying Morpheus away from Khronus's island and back to the realm of dreams.

The Morningstar's story had reached a conclusion. But with no Devil in Hell and no God in Heaven, the future remained uncertain.

AFTERWORD

Endings are always a little bittersweet. On the one hand, we tend to have a feeling of, "oh man, I wish there was more…" But on the other, sometimes characters wear our their welcome and there's a failure to recapture that old magic. As a viewer, I'm thinking of the return of *Arrested Development*.

Believe it or not, writers share that same divided opinion on endings. I've found that five to six books tends to be the sweet spot for most of my characters. Beyond that, I also start to feel like maybe it's time to try something different.

But every time when I'm in the middle of writing that final book, I start to get cold feet. "Should I really end it? Maybe there's more stuff I can do with this character?"

Ultimately, you've got to go with what's best for the character, and I feel like Lucifer's story had reached a good conclusion. When I chose Lucifer to be the subject of the first spin-off series from the Luther Cross books, I knew I wanted to do something different with the character.

I've liked some of the different interpretations I've seen of the Devil. Whether it's the calm confidence of Viggo Mortensen in *The Prophecy*, the strange mix of petulance and charm of Mark Pellegrino in *Supernatural*, the creepy scenery-chewing of Peter Stormare in *Constantine*, the amusingly approachability of Tom Ellis in *Lucifer*, or even the batshit insanity of Al Pacino in *Devil's Advocate*.

This is a character that has been interpreted and re-interpreted countless times throughout literature, film, television, video games, comics—you name it. Even by me once before in my first novel, *Fallen*.

How to set this version of Lucifer apart from all those others was the question I posed to myself. And it occurred to me that most depictions of the Devil seemed to hinge on jealousy of humanity or a sense of being betrayed by his father (i.e. God).

That made me think about the Gnostic interpretations of Christianity. In most Judeo-Christian interpretations and literature, the serpent in the story of *Genesis* is a malevolent figure, often interpreted as the Devil (or an emissary of the Devil). But the Gnostics viewed the serpent as a wise figure trying to bring knowledge to humanity and the "God" of the Old Testament as the Demiurge, a malevolent figure who had created the physical world and tried to keep humanity from attaining enlightenment.

This also made me think of similar stories in mythology, such as Prometheus in Greek mythology who tried to bring fire to mankind and was punished.

As I'm sure is no surprise to anyone who's been reading these books, I'm not a religious man. I was raised Christian, but I became agnostic in my teenage years, dabbled with Taoism and chaos magic in my twenties, and am now a card-carrying secular humanist. One of the things that always bothered me about the Christian beliefs I was raised on is the idea of that strict binary—good vs. evil just seems

226

so prosaic. The idea of a pure good and a pure evil felt unrealistic. And it's certainly not very interesting from a storytelling perspective.

This reminded me of a line from *Supernatural*, which I've mentioned before. There's a scene when Anna, the fallen angel, tells Dean that only four angels have ever actually seen God. All the other angels have to take his very existence on faith.

Anyone who has watched *Supernatural* knows that there is a real God in that show. I won't spoil it if you haven't watched the show (though if you start to watch it, you'll be able to put the clues together long before the show comes out and tells you). But I was left wondering, "what if Heaven existed…but God didn't?" That made me think of a famous quote by Voltaire—"If God did not exist, it would be necessary to invent him."

That was the key to my version of Lucifer. He wouldn't be someone who was rebelling against his father or seeking revenge for a perceived betrayal. Nothing against those stories, but they did it better than I could, so why retread the same ground?

I wanted to look at a Lucifer as a broken man. He had the loftiest of goals and, like a lot of us in our younger years, felt he could change the world. But then the world fought back and he gave up.

This series has been about a journey for Lucifer, going from someone who gave up because he felt like he wasn't given his due and that transformation into accepting that not everything was going to go his way and he didn't have all the answers.

Some people may not be happy where Lucifer ends up at the finale of this book, but to me, this was always the natural end. Lucifer's greatest adversary in the various stories has always been his own arrogant pride. That's why the ultimate enemy at the end of this book was literally himself.

Even though this is the end of Lucifer's story, the Dark Crossroads universe will live on. I've already polled readers and asked what you want to see and I was quite surprised by the results. But after two polls, the answer became clear—the character people want to see more of is Cain.

I wasn't expecting this result, but ever since I saw the poll results leaning in that direction, I started doing some research and coming up with ideas. And I think it'll be an interesting ride.

That means I'll see you soon in the *Mark of Cain* series. I hope you enjoy it and that you continue to support the Dark Crossroads books.

Perry Constantine
May 2022
Kagoshima, Japan

SEE HOW THE FALL BEGAN!

MORNINGSTAR
BOOK 0

LUCIFER
FALLEN

PERCIVAL CONSTANTINE

LUCIFER.PERCIVALCONSTANTINE.COM

Printed in Great Britain
by Amazon

21730819R00140